See No Evil

See No Evil

Marjorie Eatock

A Judy Sullivan Book
Walker and Company
New York

First published in the United States of America in 1985 by the
Walker Publishing Company, Inc.

Published simultaneously in Canada by John Wiley & Sons Canada,
Limited, Rexdale, Ontario.

Library of Congress Cataloging in Publication Data

Eatock, Marjorie, 1927–
    See no evil.

    "A Judy Sullivan book."
    I. Title.
PS3555.A75S4   1985   813'.54   85–10620
ISBN 0-8027-0862-5

Printed in the United States of America

10 9 8 7 6 5 4 3 2 1

To   *Sam, Boo, Jim, Lita, and Sonny—my resident Cubbers*
Bud and Connie
Leona and Wood
Darwin
Dick
And all else who love Cubbing in a J-3 Cub!

Chapter One

THE PILOT OF the yellow airplane had no idea a murder had just taken place in the meadow a hundred feet beneath her.

Her purpose in flying so low across the red and gold sweep of trees and pasture was to try to confirm, as quickly as possible, exactly where she was. She did not see the tall man with the knife standing astride his victim and looking up at her. She did not see the old Ford, one door hanging open, on the side of the rutted dirt road.

She had not, in fact, seen much of anything for what seemed like hours but had only been seconds before when she'd lost her glasses. At the top of an aerobatic loop, the wind had snatched them from her nose and they'd gone tumbling out the open door of the elderly Piper Cub. With her spare pair in the glove compartment of her car back at the landing field and her contact lenses unreachable in her purse, Linda Pietra could, with clarity, see only a few feet beyond her humming propeller. Past that, the world was an abstract painting, all colored blurs and soft-edged shapes.

Dandy. Just dandy, she thought. *Okay, bimbo. The glasses are gone. Forget them. Squint. Look hard.*

She saw fields and trees. Splendid. Half of Pike County was fields and trees. But hallelujah! There was the river, that blessed old gray snake of a Mississippi, lapping the pilings of the summer cottages at Cincinnati Landing and making the little, tethered boats bob like small cockleshells. Just a tad east beyond the highway was home!

She drew a sharp breath that was only partial relief. Now that she had her bearings, getting home was a snap. The next challenge would be to make a safe landing—one that in this case included staying on the narrow strip, missing the runway lights, and not rolling her precious Cubby into a shattered ball of junk.

With a sharp pang she suddenly thought of Will Westerson, who had just sold his beloved airplane to her because he couldn't afford to keep it. When he found out she'd done something so unspeakably stupid as putting the Cub in jeopardy by flying blind—that could well be the end with Will. She could almost see his tanned face setting into stone, see the level, accusing dark eyes, the grim mouth beneath the black mustache. She could also see him turn and walk away. That would hurt worse than anything he might say. Lashing out was not Will's style. He just scorched with glances. Glances, she could handle. Walking off could mean something shattered beyond repair.

Linda swallowed hard and gritted her teeth. Now was hardly the time to review her poor batting average with men. Giving herself a stern mental shake, she tried to forget Will, forget how panicky she was, forget that the two legs connecting her hips with the feet on the rudder pedals seemed to have turned into watery jello.

Concentrate, you knucklehead! You're no novice! You started flying when you were eight, sitting in your dad's lap. You have your instrument, commercial, and multiengine ratings. You bought the Cub to have fun. Relax. Have some!

She forced herself to look out at the yellow sweep of the Piper's wings, at the black-browed nose pointing calmly northeast. She listened to the steady chugging thrum of the engine. The Cub was okay. She was okay.

She just had to get them both safely on the ground.

And so far, so good. She was passing over the old abandoned airstrip on the river bluff top, where they'd made a drug bust last week. But the strip was only a checkpoint, not a temptation. No need to risk putting a gearleg in a chuckhole trying to land there. She was bound for home.

The Cub was crossing the river now, casting a small shadow on the silver-rippled water. There were the grain elevators on the other side. Fine. Now came the fuzzy brown squares of Will Westerson's bean fields. That blob of red just pulling on to the brown must be a combine—probably, with her luck, driven by Will. She already knew Will had some sort of mental radar when the Cub was flying. All she needed today was Will as an audience when she landed!

Oh dear God, let me get us down all right, she thought. It was a fervent prayer for a descent and landing that would be unremarkable to all appearances.

Discovering that the girl he'd just met was a pilot had been obviously hard for Will to take. Selling her his Cub had made another hairline crack in their tenuous relationship. And she'd liked him so much—so much—that in the ensuing weeks she'd played a coward's game, putting off mentioning that she was also an aerobatic pilot who'd flown the classic J-3 Cub comedy routine in her father's air shows for ten years. She'd known she'd have to tell him—and soon, now, since she was to fly again for her dad next week at a show too close to Will's farm to escape notice.

She had argued with herself: *It's not Will's Cub. It's my Cub. I bought it outright, with the divorce settlement from Tony Pietra.* And Will knew it was her Cub. He had never by word or glance indicated differently. Yet, because she loved it so, she knew how he had loved it; and such a love doesn't go away with a bill of sale.

So she was on a guilt trip. All right!

I had, she thought grimly, *better be on something else just now—like my toes!* Because the single runway of the home field was more or less in view, and the moment of truth was coming up fast!

She swallowed, shaking the brown swing of hair behind the kerchief to clear all silly cobwebs, wiped one hand on her jeans, dropped the Cub nose, and got down to business.

The long gray line splitting the fuzzy green-brown of autumn grass below was the strip, with a blob of buildings at one end and flanked by a pair of cars in the parking lot, also blobby. No blobs seemed to be in motion anywhere. It was, fortunately, too early in the morning for anyone else to be flying from this particular small-town airport.

Linda made one low steady pass to check the direction of the wind by the tee, climbed again, turned the yellow plane, lined it up with the fuzz of the runway and took a deep, shaky breath. Suddenly she seemed to be a bit short of air.

''Okay, sweetie,'' she said aloud to her humming yellow butterfly. ''Here we go. All or nothing!''

Back across the river in the early morning quiet of the sun-washed meadow, the murderer had stood frozen just that one long moment, staring after the receding tail of the yellow plane.

It had appeared from nowhere. Zip. There it had been, coming at his head so low and so fast that for a moment he couldn't believe his bad luck.

But believe it he must. He was a realist. He also had to admit to himself that he hadn't risen in his peculiar avocation without setbacks. He'd dealt with setbacks before, although truthfully none quite like this one. He knew nothing about aircraft. However, one point was clarion clear: His basic success lay in his anonymity, and that anonymity had just been imperiled. He had to do something about it.

In his chosen side line, the man was known simply as ''Slit.'' He had another name in what was virtually another life—with a wife and family, two cars, and a nine-to-five job. He was tall, athletic, with graying hair and a pleasant smile that stopped at his eyes. His eyes were the color of dirty ice.

There were days when well-dressed men who dealt with dark things in sunny offices would press a button on their executive desks and say with a pseudodainty reluctance, ''Gentlemen, we seem to have a job for Slit.''

On those days Slit didn't go to his nine-to-five, and there were no questions asked.

The men in the bright offices didn't know about his other name. They didn't want to know. They only knew he could use a knife quietly, neatly, and without fail. His anonymity was a great part of his reputation.

Until now.

Now. Ten years down the tube!

Slit was very angry. He knew he'd been seen at last. He'd seen her—a dumb broad with blowing brown hair, blundering across the timberline in a yellow airplane just as his knife had found its mark.

Now he had to find her.

Almost absently, and certainly with no compassion, he nudged Joey Brachetti's recumbent form with his foot, loosing a smell of bruised peppermint and wet clover. He was dead. No question he was dead.

And his own damned fault, too.

If he hadn't suddenly taken alarm, jumped from the car and gone running across this field, he'd be alive yet. At least for a while. At least until they'd reached Slit's preselected spot on the bluff top near the abandoned airstrip. Slit favored high quiet places far away from his home turf in St. Louis. The bluff top would have been perfect. Finding a stray body there wouldn't draw the attention of Lieutenant Elman, who was a smart cop. The prospect of a prime bale of Venezuelan grass was the lure Slit had offered Joey to get him to the spot—a perfect temptation for a small-time grifter like Joey, who'd cheated on his bookmaking so long he thought he could get away with anything.

But something had spooked Joey.

Oh well. No matter. It was just a lousy break. He'd had lousy breaks before, and the job was done. This one, anyway.

He bent, pulled out his knife, immune to the nasty sucking noise it made, and wiped the blade clean with a handful of dry meadow grass. A speck near the haft disturbed him. He rubbed it off, using Joey's shirtsleeve. Tools had to be treated with respect; he was trying to teach his kids that.

Then, not in haste, but wasting no time, he took Joey by his arms and dragged him over into the edge of the shade made by willows along a creek bed. That would have to do. Joey wouldn't care, anyway.

Painstakingly, he searched the dead bookmaker's pockets, taking his wallet, his credit cards, and all other means of identification. There was no point in making it too easy for the local hick cops. Then he walked briskly back to Joey's car, never noticing the warmth of the sun on his shoulders or the sweet clover beneath his feet. The Ford was still running, one door agape from Joey's sudden bolt for freedom. He slid in, tossed the little man's ballcap into the rear seat on top of his rain poncho. Joey, he thought wryly, had come prepared. Lot of good it did him.

From the back seat he retrieved Brachetti's loose-leaf account books and thumbed through them quickly. It was not so much to know the reasons for Joey's downfall as to search for information useful to himself. This morning, however, his mind wasn't on future advantages. Satisfied he had what his employers wanted, he tossed the books back to join the ballcap. The zippered bank bag of money went into an inside pocket of his own jacket, unopened. Slit was too well paid to play penny ante. Besides, his thoughts were centered on the broad in the airplane.

He had to find her. Fast. She had to die. Fast. It was as simple as that. There was no place in his cobra mind for sentiment.

He got out a road map and oriented himself, running his index finger in its skintight glove across the river. The plane had gone east. There was only one airport nearby, not counting the bluff top. It was north of a burg named Penfield. So, with luck, that's where she'd gone. It would be the nearest place to call the cops. And a broad who flew a yellow airplane shouldn't be too hard to find.

He had to find her. A shadow cannot exist when it has a face and a name. He planned to exist quite a while longer.

Joey, he didn't worry about. Joey was a cipher, rubbed out. The local cops were welcome to the erasure. It might give them something exciting to do besides chase hog stealers.

He put the car in gear, backed it around expertly, startling quail from the underbrush, and drove away as carelessly as though leaving behind a sack of garbage. His anger at the woman, at having things go wrong, began to drain from him. He felt relaxed. Confident. Joey had left behind a bag of caramels; he ate a couple as he drove toward the river. After all, how much trouble could a broad in a yellow airplane be?

The broad in the airplane was having troubles of her own. Her heart was thumping, her hand clammy cold on the stick between her knees. She squinted desperately, trying to make out the wind direction. Damn. It was right smack across the runway, and the windsock was straight out. No, it wasn't. It had dropped. But there it went again, as stiff as though it had a board through it. So the wind was blowing gusts. Big, slamming, dangerous gusts, coming right up out of the gullies.

Oh, well. She'd made crosswind landings before. Hundreds of them. But she'd almost ground-looped before, too, and that was with usable eyes! Eyes to judge her distance from the ground, eyes to see the sides of the strip!

Oh please, she breathed silently to whatever powers governed pilots and other foolish folk, *please don't let me ding up my little yellow bird!*

She was totally on her own. Nineteen-forty Cubs don't have radios, and Emergency Landing Transmitters only function on crash. Besides that, it was not even seven o'clock. The airport operator wouldn't even be around to run out and pick up the pieces.

She finished flying her base leg and turned the airplane on its final approach. Then the wind hit her, rocking the light plane sideways, making the forward biting propeller roar angrily. She shoved the nose down and squinted at the blur that was rushing up at her fast. The runway should be under her now.

She cut back on her power. Then the crimson row of warning VASI lights glared their scary message: Too low! Too low! And too short! Good God, she was about to land in Will's bean field; the plane was still a hundred feet north of the strip!

Frantically she applied power again. The Cub surged forward and up, crabbing sideways. But it climbed! It climbed!

In the air safely again, she let out her breath in a sob, leveled off, tried to regain her wits. Perhaps if she just flew around a moment. The baling wire that topped the gas float was halfway up. Fuel was no problem. *She* was the problem.

Okay. Recap the situation: The vicious gusts wouldn't let her coast in; further, they wanted to blow her right off the strip. At best it was going to be tricky for any pilot—but by golly she wasn't just any pilot! She was a damned good one! And, once she was over the strip for sure, eyes wouldn't help anyway. Her tools would be experience and instinct, and she had those!

Base leg, again. Turn on final. Last prayer. Last chance.

Easy. Easy. Damn that wind!

There. There was the runway. Now she could see it pretty well, but the wind wouldn't let her stay lined up with it. She was tossing like a leaf!

Then the wind dropped.

So did she.

The airplane bounced, slewed like a wild thing, bounced again, then came down to stay. But it was traveling almost crosswise. One gear came up off the ground—and with it Linda's heart—as the opposite wingtip dropped perilously close to the unforgiving surface of the strip. She seesawed like a beginner, playing her heel brakes frantically one against the other, avoiding a ground loop but almost going nose over in the process. In a sort of heartsick litany she was saying, *Please God, please, God . . .*

The wind stayed down. The Cub straightened out, began to

slow its pell-mell roll. The only noise was its steadily chugging engine—and the frantic thump of her own heart.

She slowly churned her way up the taxi strip. Her usual tie-down spot was near the end of the row, next to a dew-bright and stately old Stinson. She swung the tail around, cut the power, leaned back against the cool seat, and shut her eyes. Then suddenly they popped open again. For the very first time it occurred to her—something else besides the Piper Cub could have been hurt out there. That something was Linda Pietra.

Granted, few women she knew had managed to ball up their lives quite as expertly as she in the past two years, but she'd never had a death wish. And she didn't have one now.

She wanted to live. She wanted this small town to like the new girl at the Farm Bureau office, she wanted to hold on to those tentative beginnings with Will Westerson and make them lasting. She'd never realized how badly she wanted those things until now, with the knowledge that she'd been within one flicker of losing everything.

She shut her eyes again, limp, and not a little sick. She let the cool October air dry the sweat on her round face, ruffle the clammy sweep of brown hair behind the scarlet scarf. She swallowed, resolutely willing the nausea to subside.

She'd made it. She and Cubby. Perhaps it was a sign. Perhaps now the only way was up.

Then she heard feet. Beyond the crackle and creak of the old engine cooling she heard them. Cracking across the concrete. Coming closer. Authoritative feet.

She knew who it was. She knew in her soul. And she did not want to open her eyes. She wasn't ready.

It didn't matter. The feet had arrived, ready or not. And a deep, hard, rather acid voice inquired brutally, ''What the holy hell did you think you were doing out there?''

Will Westerson. Of course. Naturally. Who else?

She gritted her teeth against the shaking, opened her eyes, and found Will's, very gray and very cold and hardly a foot away as he stood at the open door of the plane glaring at her. Ex-St. Louis policeman, neophyte farmer, Will was broad-chested, stocky, built like a brick wall, and used to command. It all showed.

Linda had been ready to cry. Now her mouth clamped shut; she swallowed again and answered very carefully, "There's a mean crosswind."

"Crosswind, hell! First you come across low, scaring the juice out of my heifers, then you peel up, come around again and damn near wipe out the fence line with your gear!"

Calm, Linda. Calm. "I'm sorry. I lost my glasses flying."

"You lost your—"

He stopped. His square face tightened with something different, something indefinable. "Good grief, woman! You mean you couldn't see?"

She shook her head. The tears were coming back, and they mustn't. She couldn't let him see her cry; she wasn't ready to show this man her unprotected side. "N—not very well."

The small stutter broke his anger, touching him. "Linda, for God's sake!" and his brown, calloused hand went from gripping the door to her ruffling hair, stroking it gently. His voice had suddenly come from the depth of his chest. Her breath stopped, because at last, after two long months of casual nothing, at last there might be something, just the delicate silk of something between them, something that said, *Go on, cry, with this man it will be all right.*

Then his eyes caught the flutter of paper taped to the in-strument panel. She saw them widen, then turn almost black, the softness gone, the ebony frozen. He reached out, tore the paper loose. His voice grated across that frail silk, tearing it with words. "What the hell's this? Chandelle. Spin. Inside loop. Good gravy! No wonder you lost your glasses. I'd say you lost your marbles, too! What have you been doing with my air-plane?"

Her eyes stung, but the tears were angry ones now. She

reached out, snatched her penciled aerobatic routine from him, defiantly stuck it back on the panel. Coldly she snapped, because she hurt, "It's not your airplane!"

Then she could have bitten her tongue, would have done almost anything to take back those hasty words.

But she couldn't. Neither could she bring herself to explain. If there was an explanation. Perhaps there wasn't.

For a moment, a brief moment, he stared frozen, the tragedy in his eyes that only another pilot who'd parted with a well-loved aircraft could understand. Then the heavy shoulders inside the denim jacket sagged, and he looked away. From the plane. Mostly from her. And in that look she saw everything that had almost started slip away again, too.

Quietly he answered, "You're right. I'm sorry. I was out of line. I'm glad you weren't hurt. Help you tie down?"

"No. Thank you." She was shaking, so she didn't want him to see her climb out; she might fall. And she wanted nothing—nothing—that might be construed as a feminine trick, a wile, to regain his sympathy.

He shrugged. He was still looking away. "Okay. Suit yourself."

She watched him go back across the concrete, through the brown mustard weed along the fence row, throw a leg over the top wire, and climb up into the red grain truck parked alongside. Far across the sere brown ranks of soybeans, the combine was approaching, chuffing, sucking up beans, blowing out chaff.

Will was a farmer now. Not a pilot. Not a cop. Bone and soul weary of the dark side of police work, he had made this choice when his father's death had left him the rundown farm. But something had to go to help pay for that combine and a new tractor and a spreader and a thousand other things. Something like a yellow 1940 J-3 Piper Cub.

Linda shut her eyes again, drawing a ragged breath.

Why did it have to be so tough? Why couldn't two lonely

people find each other without all this extraneous detail, without kicking at each other's toys like spoiled kids?

At a low point, herself; weary, disillusioned, and insecure from two years in the fast lane with her freewheeling ex-husband, Linda had taken a job in this small town for a respite, for re-evaluation. A month after she'd arrived, a burly arm had flopped two beer cans filled with soil samples on her Farm Bureau desk, and she'd glanced up for the first time at Will Westerson.

He'd looked like any other young farmer in a tractor cap, except he'd been quieter. Older. A little more wary. That had been all right. So was she. It probably set them apart from the other more easygoing people as much as being the two new kids on the block. It was also probably the reason they'd hit it off so well. She'd learned, piece by piece, that a mounting intolerance with the human race had taken him out of police work and back to the farm. He'd learned, with equal casualness, that she was recently divorced from an airline pilot and had come to Penfield hoping a new job and a new environment would help her get her act together. Neither knew the other flew until the fateful day he mentioned having to sell his Cub, and with her ex-husband Tony's money burning in her pocket, she had bought it.

She certainly had. And nothing had been quite the same between them since, of that she was sure. What she didn't know was the reason. Was it because she was a woman pilot, or that she was a woman pilot flying his airplane? Neither of those reasons? Both of them? Or merely that she'd come on to him too fast, threatened his independence? She hadn't meant to do that!

But it was downright chicken of her not to tell Will she was going to fly the Cub in her father's air show. She couldn't deny that. Now he'd find out the wrong way, and no matter what she did, it was going to be wrong, too. She had to admit that in the back of her head she'd dreamed of Will being in the audience, watching her, disguised as a little old lady, pretending that the

cub was taking off without a pilot and her a helpless passenger.
She'd imagined the wild swoops and loops she'd do, seeing his
grin at her screams of "Save me!" Then when the crowd realized they'd been had, she'd pull up into a falling leaf and land
to applause and laughter. It was a fun routine, and fun to prac-
tice—until this morning. Her very first thought this morning
when she woke was of her bowling date with Will for Friday.
Now he was mad. And it all might be over.

"Damn," she whispered, indulging in a little self-pity. Just
when things had been going fairly well!

Perhaps that was it. The clue. When things do go well, look
out!

To that philosophic thought she said a word closely connected with her current agricultural associations, unsnapped her
belt, and climbed stiffly out. The Cub's load lightened, thirty
feet of yellow wing began to rock in the gusting wind. She
grabbed a tie-down ring and stooped, scrabbling for the long
coiled rope at her feet. A cheery voice called, "I'll get the
other."

Glancing beneath the nose she caught a quick glimpse of the
skinny denim legs and runover sneakers of Tommy, the line
boy. "Thanks," she answered.

He tied the tail, too, then came around to her side, wearing
his usual freckle-faced grin. "There we go. A Thomas Special. I
saw you come down. Some fun."

She shook her head. "Wow. And the windsock was dead on
its hanger when I took off. You liked my landing?"

"I have seen," he replied generously, "better. Maybe not as
exciting, but definitely better. Can I bum a ride to town? I
missed the school bus."

"Sure. The Cub needs fuel."

"I'll gas her tonight. The boss has a charter trip, so I'll be
here until eight this week."

Linda nodded, reaching back into the plane. "Fine. Just
make out a fuel ticket, then. Here. Haul these things to the car.
I'll be there in a minute. I have to make a phone call."

"Sure thing." He took her flight computer and her small camera. "Been taking pictures?"

"No. It's empty. I keep forgetting to get film."

He nodded, jogged off toward the small gate in the chainlink fence. Digging for change, she headed for the metal-hooded telephone. Charley Jackson owned that land where she'd lost her glasses. It was a very slim chance, but if Charley or one of his six sons happened to walk that particular meadow deer hunting, it wouldn't hurt to have them keep their eyes open. A hundred-and-twenty-five-dollar pair of glasses was no small loss—although she had to admit it ranked pretty far down her list of woes today.

She caught a glimpse of her wind-blown hair and squinting eyes in the shiny phone hood and shook her head in dismay. So much for the gorgeous female-in-distress syndrome, at least as it applied to her. She looked like Olive Oyl.

She said the agricultural word again, and dialed her number.

Neither Tom nor Linda paid particular attention to the old, nondescript Ford pulling into the airport parking lot. But the driver with the cold, cobra-hooded eyes saw them, and he was smiling.

Chapter Two

THE MAN IN the Ford parked near the fence. Leaving his engine running, he leaned his folded arms on the steering wheel and stared out the windshield like any casual passerby looking at airplanes.

But his eyes were not casual. *Bingo*, he thought.

That was her, just coming away from the yellow plane. A kid was with her. Carrying stuff out of the airplane. Damn. He didn't need a jerky kid to complicate things.

Where was she going?

To the telephone. Well, that was predictable. The breaks. Twenty minutes and there'd be hick cops swarming all over that field. It couldn't be helped.

Joey wouldn't mind, he thought wryly, and unwrapped another caramel.

Now his cold eyes followed the skinny kid. Where was he going?

Out the gate. To that dark blue Chevy.

Then he realized part of what the kid carried. A camera. A camera! Did she take his picture?

His knees tensed. He realized something else—the impulse was no good. Strictly amateur. The smart thing was to sit tight. Watch. Now he'd have to get both the girl and the camera. But one would probably not be far from the other. No sweat. Not yet.

The jerky kid was sitting in the car, waiting. And here she came across the walk and out the gate. Brown hair, shiny, lifting in the wind. Cream-colored silk shirt, brown slacks, nice figure. She stopped at the car door, took out a brown blazer jacket, shrugged it on. The kid handed her something from the glove compartment. Glasses. She stuck them on her face, got in, started the engine.

Slit assessed the situation swiftly, dismissed the idea of running her off the road on the way to town. Not with the jerky kid. It was easier and surer to work a nice simple fatal accident with one, not two. Patience. He had plenty of time.

She drove down the airport drive, stopped, and turned left toward Penfield.

Casually, he put his own car in reverse, started to back—

Crash!

What the hell was that? It sounded like he'd hit a whole shelf of pop cans! Cursing, he jammed the gear into park, slid out, loped around to his trunk, and looked.

A trash can lid—blown off the row of trash cans and a little bent from hitting his hubcap—lay where it had bounced back on the concrete. He kicked it out of the way viciously, got back into the Ford, and drove off. Damn. He was really in trouble if he'd lost her. . . .

He hadn't. There she was up ahead, stuck behind a jogging farm tractor.

He laid back, let an impatient Dodge get between them and drove forty miles an hour the short distance into town.

Back in the beanfield, sitting behind the wheel of the grain truck—paid for with Cub money, he was reminding himself grimly—Will Westerson had been holding on to that wheel as though the wind was trying to blow him away. He didn't realize he was holding on. He didn't actually realize he wasn't moving. His mind was too busy conducting a brisk cold war between self-pity and self-loathing, neither of which made William Woodrow Westerson look particularly great.

The Cub was not his airplane. Not anymore. He'd sold it. His own decision. No one had twisted his arm.

And she was not his girl. He had a girl—back in St. Louis. She was a cop, too. A good one. Her name was Doris Murphy, and he went down to see her sometimes. Not often. And she never came up here. Doris was a city girl—cows scared her, pigs smelled, and there were only one or two places to eat out in Penfield. Anyway, the bottom line was: He had a girl. When he wanted one.

So what the hell was he so bugged about?

He was working too hard. That was it. He should take some time off, run down to St. Louis, visit Elman and the boys at the precinct, catch Doris between airline pilots and take her out.

But he couldn't. This was his first crop year; he had to meet bank payments big enough to throttle a mule. Also, the beans had to be picked before it rained again or he'd lose them.

After the crops were in, then. There. That was decided.

So why didn't he feel better?

It was his turn for the agriculture-related word, accompanied by a smart thump on the wheel with one doubled fist.

He knew why. It was because between him and the approaching combine he kept seeing a nice, round face beneath tousled hair—a face with scared eyes, then hurt eyes after he'd stabbed her right between them with his damned big mouth!

The problem went beyond that. He'd found himself remembering her at other times, too—and more than just her face. Like when, fresh and scrubbed from the shower, he climbed into his empty bed, his cold bed, and remembered Linda Pietra's smooth round curve of hip and breast, the smell of her when they slow danced, and the amber gleam through dark lashes when he couldn't get the barbecue fire to burn at the Fall Festival.

He'd lived alone out at his place for almost a year, happy as a clam, rejoicing in real trees and fresh air and friendly folks whose smiles didn't mean someone else had a bead on your backside while they conned you! Then along comes this one-hundred-pound cupcake, quiet and sweet-lipped and shy as a doe from being racked around by some airlines hotshot, and suddenly he's feeling downright deprived!

"Damn!" he said out loud. The steering wheel took a second whack. He'd never regarded himself as brilliant, but he had thought he possessed if not good sense, at least perspective! Ho, ho, ho—so much for that idea. Anyone who'd shoot off his mouth to a nice girl like Linda as he'd just done had the outlook of a cross-eyed moose.

So she was a pilot! So were lots of other women—good pilots.

But they weren't flying his airplane.

That was the point, it wasn't his airplane.

He knew her dad was an ex-airline jock, running a little airport on a shoestring somewhere out in Kansas. She'd told him that. He should have realized Daddy's Little Girl wouldn't be content to just fly nice and level from Point A to Point B. She'd probably been doing loops since she was three—and damned good ones!

Envy. That's the problem—pure envy of something he'd never had a chance to do, and now with a farm around his neck probably never would.

But you chose the farm, bucko. Don't take it out on your girl.

The fist suddenly smacked again—the third and last time.

''She's not my girl!'' he snarled aloud, started the truck, and backed it around to be in position to load from the combine.

That was when he heard the tin crash of the garbage can lid.

He raised up, craned his neck, and was just in time to witness a tall guy get out of an old Ford at the airport fence, apply foot to trash lid, get back in, and drive off.

Short-fused character. Nobody he knew.

Or—was it?

Had he seen him before?

Not around these parts.

Maybe St. Louis.

Where, in St. Louis?

Doing what?

And, if he was from St. Louis, what was he doing at a pipsqueak airport this early in the morning?

Oh, for cryin' out loud, Will said to his eternal cop men-

But it teased him all morning—the big, athletic frame, the catlike movement, the stony profile.

He knew him, all right. From somewhere or something.

No matter. He'd remember. He always did.

At least it was better than thinking about Linda.

Slit's interest quickened as Linda dropped Tom off at the high school. A lot of accidents can happen in a big school complex. When neatly arranged. But she didn't stop there. She drove to the edge of town and went into a fast-food place.

Incredible. The dumb broad has just seen a murder and she has time to snarf up biscuits! But that was somewhat besides the point. The point was that she'd left the camera in the car.

He parked far back in the lot, still able to keep both her and her car in view. Eyes narrowed, he assessed the situation briefly.

Not good. Her Chevy was flanked by a pickup truck and a Dodge—both occupied. With kids. That was worst of all. Kids never missed a thing. He'd just have to take a chance and wait. The big window poster of scrambled eggs and sausage didn't bother him. He never ate much when he was hunting. He did unwrap another caramel and chewed it thoughtfully, watching her through the plate glass.

A lot of people going in and out. There's money in those fast-food jobs. His wife thought so; her friend Marcia managed one. The whole nation, Marcia said, is freaked out on junk food. Not him. He was a meat-and-potatoes man.

The Dodge pulled out. Slit considered moving in alongside the Chevy and decided against it. The yard apes were still in the pickup truck; besides he really didn't want to get that close to his quarry. Not yet.

Soon enough.

Suddenly his belly tightened. He went rigid in the seat, his face a hard mask.

A state trooper had come in the opposite door. He could see him clearly—a big dude, and excited as hell. He was hailing down the girl!

He made a lightning decision: Wait. Stay cool.

That's when you shot rabbits—when they broke cover and ran.

He was no damned rabbit.

He was not conscious of flicking his tongue along his lips. Like a snake. He only knew that the one person in the world who could truly finger him was talking to a cop.

The conversation was brief.

The trooper turned, bolted back out the door. In a moment his state patrol car came barreling around the corner. It passed the Ford, made a left turn, squealed toward town.

Flick. Flick. The tongue on dry lips.

Then the girl—she came running out, carrying a coffee cup.

She never looked his way. She got in her Chevy, backed it out, and followed the trooper.

He exhaled one short gasp of air.

Well. Some sort of fat was in the fire, and he thought he knew whose. His.

Dumb broad, he said to himself, *you should have handed over the camera when you had a chance. . . .*

He joined the traffic flow right behind her. He was just a shade anxious. That camera bugged him. But luck was still his. She only followed the police car a block or so before she abruptly turned south. So. Maybe she'd been told to go home. Dandy. He'd like that a lot. He could handle people in their homes. It was usually like shooting fish in a barrel.

She slowed up and flashed her right-turn signal. He slowed, too, and watched.

There was a big old white house surrounded by tall trees whose leaves were turning red and gold and making a mess on the lawn. Slit had no trees at his house—just a low, neat hedge. Rigidly clipped. The woman pulled up into a side drive beneath the trees, hurried across the lawn and up onto the porch. He could see plainly, she didn't even unlock—she just opened the door and went in!

Jeez! Small town hicks were so dumb that they begged for trouble! He and Mona never left their door unlocked! Never! Even the kids had to ring the bell.

It was an apartment house. He discovered that as he cruised by. Four mailboxes. Okay. No sweat. Up the street her neighbors were getting out stuff for a yard sale. Three or four cars were already parked waiting, and more were pulling in. He joined them, parking Joey's Ford facing the girl's place. Then he sat quietly, deliberating. Absently, his tongue licked at the caramel on his teeth.

He liked night best. But he couldn't wait for night. Not handily. He'd like to hit and get gone. It was his wedding anniversary and he had forgotten to order flowers. He always gave Mona flowers. And diamonds. When she'd been good. He'd find a pay phone somewhere in this dumpy town and use Joey's credit card.

In the meantime, there were many ways of getting into an apartment. In fact, all she needed to do was open the door to him. His "partner" was silent. Very. Joey had found that out.

He was to discover shortly, however, that Linda was going to be a bit more difficult. On the way to town she'd made cheerful conversation with Tom using only half her mind; the other half was licking its wounds. Her thoughts were doing circles around two things: Will and the Cub. She could sell the Cub, get a Citabria or a Pitts—some high-performance bumblebee that would make the Cub look like a lazy butterfly. But she'd flown Cubs for years, and she loved this one.

That was the problem, of course. Will Westerson loved it too. She'd told him he was welcome to fly it anytime, but his pride was obviously too damned stiff. If she flew some other airplane, would he still mind? If she flew some other airplane, then could she keep Will? Did Will want to be kept? Figuratively, of course! And, even more serious, what was it about the man that made her want to keep him, that would make life in this little town without him so hollow she'd want to move on again?

She'd never wanted for dates. But she'd never cared that much about having them either. Tony had been different. For a while. But the bad taste from that marriage had left her disinterested in anything in a moustache, so she thought.

Until Will.

"North door," said Tommy, startling her.

"North door?"

"Yeah, let me out at the north door. I have P.E. first hour and that's closest to the lockers."

"Oh. All right."

She double-parked briefly, behind a station wagon disgorging bright pom-poms with girls underneath. Tom hopped out, saying, "I put your camera in the back on the seat."

"Thanks. There's no film in it; I just kept forgetting to take it out of the plane. Have a good day, Tom."

"You, too. I'll gas the Cub as soon as I get out there."

"No problem. I won't fly again until tomorrow, anyway. Tom—"

"Yeah?"

"Do you know anyone who might want to buy her?"

"The Cub? You want to sell Will's plane?"

Then he reddened, mumbled, "Sorry. Dumb question."

"I," she said crisply, "am thinking about a hotter plane—a Citabria. Or a Pitt. An Eagle, maybe."

"Oh." His polite tone indicated his was not to reason why. "I don't know offhand of anyone. But I'll ask around. Do you want me to put a sign on it?"

She hesitated. A sign would be a commitment, and she really hadn't thought it through. "No. Maybe just something on the bulletin board."

"Okay. Thanks for the ride. 'Bye." He loped off after the perambulating pom-poms.

Linda glanced at her watch. Seven-thirty, and the day had already been rather lumpy. She'd better get something in her stomach. Perhaps a quick coffee and Danish with her very pregnant friend Sue before she went to work. And Sue was pretty sharp. Maybe she'd have some answers.

However, Sue—who managed the fast-food place on the edge of town—was not managing any fast food that day. Sue had, a bright young girl in an orange uniform told her excitedly, gone to deliver something far more important than a double cheeseburger.

Linda had just paid for her coffee when Sue's husband roared in the door. Ronnie was very large and very flustered and had his state trooper hat on backward. He had also been looking high and low for Linda.

"Here I am," Linda said, "What can I do to help?"

"Would you go by the apartment and feed Pussycat? He wasn't back when we had to leave, and Linda, you know how Sue . . . worries"

Privately, Linda thought Sue might possibly have other things on her mind at the moment besides one raffish tomcat. Nevertheless, she nodded. "Of course. I'll be glad to do it."

"He knows you. That will help. I'll call you at the Farm Bureau when it happens. Oh gosh, Linda—where did I leave my car?"

"Out there," Linda answered and pointed helpfully. "Go along, Ron! I'll stop by right now and take care of his Nibs."

"Thanks," he said over his shoulder, and shot back out the door.

The girl in orange was laughing. "Lucky you," she said. "I'd rather feed a piranha. You heard what he did to the trash man?"

Linda had heard. There had been an unfortunate dispute over a turkey skeleton. Pussycat had retired victorious, not only with his booty but also with an amazing amount of skin from the trash man's hand. Pussycat was now confined to a styrofoam carrier on trash days.

She told the waitress cheerfully, "He's not so bad. All you have to do is exactly what he wants."

"Spoiled?"

"Rotten."

"How's he going to feel about the new baby?"

Linda shrugged. "He'll probably let them keep it for a pet."

In the meantime, the morning was going fast. If she was to stop by Sue's, she'd better hurry. She asked for a cap for her cup, went out holding the coffee carefully in one hand, and drove to her friends' apartment. Sue and Ron had the left half of the main floor of a lovely old house—a space, Linda guessed, that would soon become more than a little crowded.

She got out of her car and scuffed through a royal carpet of scarlet and gold provided by towering maple trees. The same wind that had sent her sideways down the runway now teased her hair lightly as she mounted the old white steps, bringing a smudgy scent of bonfires—and apples. Someone was baking apples.

The smell of cinnamon was strong in the foyer, where the polished oak stairs curved upward around a rather splendid old brass chandelier. Linda sniffed appreciatively. It must be little old Mrs. Thomas in the right-hand apartment because it certainly wasn't Sue. Not today.

She opened the door to Sue's apartment, fully prepared to receive thirty pounds of cat full on the chest.

She didn't.

Pussycat, in fact, was not even there.

Chapter Three

"DRAT," SAID LINDA softly. Nothing so far had gone right. There was no help for it; she'd just have to come back. Making one last try, she called in her most dulcet tones, "Here, Pussycat, come here, Pussycat. Chow time. Eats. Yum, yum."

Nothing. Not a sound. And she didn't want to open a tin of cat food just to let it sit around in a warm apartment all day. Sue expected a new baby, not a cat with ptomaine. Perhaps she could run back in on her lunch hour—if she ever got herself to work!

Strange how an empty apartment echoes. The wind was rattling the old windows. A brown strand of ivy scratched a pane as she walked by, making her jump. Sue's kitchen was a picture of arrested motion—popped up toast still in the toaster, bacon shoved to one side of a very cold skillet, eggs in a saucepan, now very chill and very done.

And absolutely no Pussycat.

She went to the back entrance, opened it, and looked out on a neat row of apple trees, a few windfalls making scarlet dollops on the fading grass. Three white slips whipped into snowy banners next to Mrs. Thomas's billowing Victorian nightgown on the one long clothesline. Two trash cans lined up like Tweedledum and Tweedledee. Ron's half-restored 1932 Model A, swathed in a canvas drop cloth splotched pink and blue from painting the nursery. Leaves, scudding into crisp windrows.

No Pussycat.

"Okay, buddy, tough cheese," said Linda to the absent feline. She closed the kitchen door behind her, walked around the corner of the house, got in her Chevy, and left for work by driving straight on through to the alley and cutting across to Washington Street.

Had she known about the tall man in the Ford, or if she'd wanted to elude him, she couldn't have done it better. What she really intended to do was dodge two stoplights and avoid being late for work. At least—very late. She did want to put in her contact lenses.

Two of her coworkers were in the Farm Bureau washroom giggling over a packet of photographs.

"Hi, Lin, come see these! They're neat!"

"They're the ones I took at the Fall Festival," Vivian explained. Vivian was rotund and rosy; she and her husband Clyde had helped Linda and Will at the Farm Bureau barbecue tent. "Look, there's Clyde at the bean pot. And here's you and Will. Now isn't that darling? I told you it would be a cute picture."

Cute being a relative term, Linda thought wryly. The photograph showed her and Will wearing their official *Hogs Are Beautiful* T-shirts, Will's stretched across his deep chest. They were standing, per instruction, beneath the banner asking, "Have you hugged your pig today?" and Will had one big arm self-consciously around her shoulders. But he was smiling. Linda, looking at that tanned, black-moustached face, felt her heart melt, remembering.

That had been the first night he'd kissed her. It had been tentative and very light; he'd said something banal about thanks for a nice evening and quickly retreated down the steps to his pickup truck.

She'd stayed leaning against her front door, watching his retreating red taillights with eyes that hadn't seen, conscious only of the thundering of her heart, remembering the smell and feel and bulk and warmth of that one quick embrace. She'd been incredulous at her reaction. She'd believed that, after Tony, the capacity was gone. She'd walked at last into her own living room and sat down. As she stared at the furnishings so carefully chosen to be impersonal, requiring neither love nor care, she could feel the change. The cold protective sheath around her soul was cracking, and she knew it. The time had come to let it crack.

She *could* let someone else in. She *could* try again.

That night she'd unpacked two much-loved pictures and hung them on the living room walls. She'd gone back downstairs and picked the last of the creamy tea roses by the light of the moon to put in her mother's Waterford crystal vase. She went to bed with a suddenly serene feeling of—being home.

And now—looking at the snapshots—it all came back.

The cause was Will Westerson. She wanted him. She wanted him badly. And what had she done to further her cause?

She'd bought his stupid airplane, that was what! And now it looked as though the chances of ever sharing it graciously with him had all disappeared!

Mumbling inanities, she gave back the photograph and bent over the washbasin to pop in her contacts. Behind her, Vivian said, ''Smile!'' As she peered around with the half-witted look anyone has who is putting in contact lenses, Vivian's camera flashed.

''There!'' Vivian said with satisfaction. ''That's the last on the roll. Anyone going to town at noon? I'd like to get these dropped off at the finisher's.''

''I am,'' said Linda a bit acidly, and put the completed film in her blazer pocket. ''Are the rest as charming as the one you just took?''

''Of course. To me, anyway. They're mostly Jeffy with his face in his first birthday cake. Nine o'clock, kiddies. Face the public time!''

Linda got herself through the morning routine with one eye on the clock, ears tuned to the telephone, and only half a heart. Over and over she kept seeing Will's face as he'd recognized that piece of paper on the Cub panel for what it was: an aerobatic routine. How could she tell him she wasn't imperiling the Cub, that she was actually good, without sounding like a braggart?

When she got back in her car at twelve, she had a hammering headache. That darned Pussycat better be home, and he'd better not give her any lip!

A great part of Slit's success was that he was a patient man, almost totally in control of his own emotions. He sat in the Ford for quite a while, exhibiting no outward signs of restlessness, making no motions that drew attention to himself. Around him traffic increased, the parking places filled up, and people in ones, twos, threes, even sixes, slammed doors, left sweaters behind as the morning warmed, and drifted toward the yard sale. At last, without hurry, he left his own car and sauntered over to the long, high-piled tables.

Junk. That's what it was—junk. Last year's clothes, jumbles of paperback novels, baby gear, a bunch of pink glassware, old magazines, quite a few appliances of questionable quality, and —on a flatbed trailer—some pieces of halfway decent furniture, although mostly Grand Rapids stuff. Kitsch and repros, his wife would say. Mona's taste ran to authentic Queen Anne. Mona's taste, as a matter of fact, was expensive in every area. Which was one reason her husband pursued his grim sideline.

He mingled with a few other bargain hunters by a rack of hunting clothes, edging unobtrusively toward the sidewalk that led to the broad's apartment. Around him the assembly grew, swelled by a dozen or so farmer-types in red Massey-Ferguson caps. Their grain trucks halted by a malfunction in the city scales, they wandered across two backyards to join the milling crowd. *Stupid cow jockeys,* Slit thought, contemptuous of their well-washed jeans and faded shirts. Then casualness fled. A sudden slam of instinct had him swinging his back to the whole group. He didn't question, he just acted. Then, only then, he thought, *I know that turkey in the blue shirt—I know him from somewhere! It's time to fade, man . . .*

He picked up a piece of pink glass, put it down, and stepped to the other side of the rack of hunting clothes, then behind a tall old armoire on the flatbed trailer. The rest was easy. All he

had to do was keep to the streetside of a whole row of pickup
trucks with camper tops.

Who the hell was that guy?

And what rotten luck!

Well. He couldn't worry about it now. He'd just been hit
with a piece of luck even more rotten! The damned broad's car
was gone.

Jesus. What a morning!

But one thing was for sure—she had to come home again
sometime.

Casually, he mounted the front steps, opened the door,
stepped inside, closed it behind him.

The foyer was empty.

Very good. In fact, perfect.

The two nameplates on the oak stairs said "Vacant" and
"Mr. James Curry." Neither one of them his quarry. The right-
hand ground-floor door proclaimed in neat brass, "Colonel and
Mrs. Benjamin Thomas, Retired." His broad was a little young
to be retired. The left-hand door said "Mr. and Mrs. Ron
Bellam."

That had to be it.

He glanced around. The foyer was quiet, no noise coming
from anywhere. A few rays of morning sun glanced off the brass
chandelier on to worn black and white tiles. Below the polished
curve of the staircase, a hanging basket of some sort of greenery
trailed long fronds down toward an old pier table. The air was
stuffy with an overlay of cinnamon. And nobody was around.
That was the important thing.

He drew on a pair of thin, silky gloves and tried the left-hand
doorknob. It turned at his touch. Unlocked.

Jeez. These hicks!

Slowly, slowly, he edged the heavy door inward.

Nobody.

Silent as a shadow he moved his big body inside with the
litheness of a cat, closing the door behind him. It made the
barest "click."

This was her apartment all right. There was a picture of her framed on a table. So far, so good.

On soft, crepe-soled feet he checked the place out. There was a living room, kitchen, bath, and two bedrooms. The kitchen was a disaster area. The living room was too open, no real place of concealment. Bathrooms made cleanup easy with plenty of water to wash off blood; however, this time, he didn't figure on having to clean up.

He recrossed the shag carpeting, took a look at the smaller bedroom, dismissed it. Some amateur had been laying on the pink and blue paint. The other one was better. It had a closet on the far side with a door that was not reflected in the dressing-table mirror. He went back into the living room, considered standing behind the front door, dismissed it. Too chancy. The closet was best. At least for a start. He always played things by ear, anyway.

He picked up the framed picture. That was her, all right. Down in the corner it said, ''Love, Linda.'' So her name was *Linda*. Okay. On a tombstone it was as good as any.

Then he froze.

There were footsteps on the porch and voices. Two people —maybe three. Entering the foyer. Silently, like a ghost, he slipped across the carpet, into the bedroom, and opened the closet door.

Encountering a rack of hanging clothes, he put one hand to push them over and one foot inside.

It was a large foot and it encountered something soft.

Instantly there rose to the heavens an insane yowl of outraged pain, and something enormous and furry clawed up his pants leg inflicting grievous injury at every lunging hold. The monster reached his chest before he could wrench it away and throw the spitting demoniacal bundle far into the living room.

Then he closed the door and huddled far back to the right, stifling his dismay, striving to govern his anger, organizing himself, even as he felt blood oozing through his shirt front and dripping from his lacerated hand.

Pussycat, landing with a solid "chunk" against the living-room wall, immediately launched himself in a furry parabola back toward the enemy, meeting only the closed closet door. This time, a little dazed, he picked himself up.

Having been inadvertently shut in the closet on his owners' somewhat hasty departure that morning, he'd first sung his outrage vehemently. Then realizing, perforce, this virtuosity had been directed toward an empty apartment, he'd curled up and gone insouciantly to sleep—slumbering, as a matter of fact, through Linda's earlier visit.

Later, his acute ears had detected another presence in the bedroom. He'd been primed for escape, ready to forgive in exchange for breakfast, when Slit had stepped on his paw.

So, when the front door opened and Linda came in, he was not predisposed to forgiveness. He was wounded, he was hungry, things were not right in this apartment, and she may as well learn it right now!

Chapter Four

WILL WESTERSON WAS not really one for yard sales, but it was something to do while he waited for the scales to be repaired; besides, there was a table set up with home-baked goodies on it and breakfast had been a long time ago.

He chowed down on half a dozen chocolate-chip cookies, then, glancing around for something to drink, his eye casually fell on a tall guy standing by the depression glass. Hey, the fellow at the airport, wasn't it? Sure it was. Same big build, same light jacket, same dark glasses. He'd picked up a piece of pink glass, put it down, turned away. Will moved toward him, not knowing why. Not knowing why at all. All sorts of characters showed up at yard sales.

Then, as luck would have it, two fellows carrying a hump-backed trunk edged between them, and by the time Will had squeezed past, the guy was gone.

But his car wasn't. He could see the old Ford, parked between two pickups.

Curious, idly annoyed at himself for being so, still sensing that somewhere he'd seen that dude before and not under pleasant circumstances, Will moved on down the line to the table of crockery.

One thing that had carried him through more than ten years of copping had been his instinct. It was bleeping now, full blast. Not quite certain why, and feeling a bit foolish, he picked up—very gingerly—the piece of pink glass the big man had handled and paid the lady in charge of the table seven dollars for it. Refusing her aid, he carefully placed it himself in the center of a box lid she gave him. He might be loony as a hoot owl, but he also might be crazy like a fox.

A chirpy voice at his elbow said, "Good morning, Will. That's a nice piece of cranberry glass."

He looked down and saw Mrs. Thomas smiling up through her wire-rimmed glasses. He smiled back. She and Ben were a neat couple, with an apartment full of Benares brass and Indian madras; Ben had "flown the Hump" during World War II and then stayed attached to the Bombay legation for the rest of his career. He smiled at her, "Good morning. My mother collects this," lying through his teeth of course, but the real explanation would be worse.

She went on, "I just bought a box of Fiesta ware. Ben will have a fit, but our daughter-in-law loves it. Will, could you carry it across the street for me? I'll give you a cup of coffee."

He glanced across the lots, saw the trucks still not moving, and said, "Sure. I'd be glad to." Balancing his own box lid on top of her treasures, he followed her across to the other curb, passing right by the old Ford.

It was still empty. A half-eaten bag of caramels lay on the seat. The front license plate was covered with mud. Casually he rubbed it with his denim knee.

Missouri license plates. And a torn bumpersticker with the name of a company in St. Louis. St. Louis, by all that was holy!

Who the hell was that dude?

Then he had it—almost. Not quite. It was like grasping at smoke . . .

Mrs. Thomas, trotting ahead, called "There's Linda!"

He turned, and everything went out of his mind because there she was indeed, getting out of her car, pulling off her brown blazer, and tossing it into the back, waving across the street and waiting for them. It could be love or it could be just plain old chemistry, but whatever it was, his heart was beating like a seventeen-year-old kid's. What a screwed-up world!

"Hi," she said. "It looks as if you made quite a haul."

Mrs. Thomas answered, "There was some of that cobalt blue Fiesta that my daughter-in-law loves. What's the word on Sue?"

Linda held the foyer door open for them. "Nothing, yet. I

just went by the hospital and found Ron chewing the furniture in the waiting room. I told him to call here until one o'clock. I'm supposed to be feeding Pussycat, but I couldn't find him this morning.''

She hardly had the words out before an outraged feline squall came from the Bellam apartment. Mrs. Thomas grinned. ''Looks like you've found him now.''

Linda swung the apartment door open. There on the shag carpet stood a monster black-and-white cat with enormous whiskers, ragged ears, and glittering green eyes. His fur was fluffed, ears laid back, and he was fizzing like a soda bottle.

Mrs. Thomas, peering beneath Will's arm, observed, ''He's mad.''

''He's hungry,'' said Linda. Her head still pounded; she resented the way the sight of Will Westerson made her stupid heart join the beat, and her voice was short. ''Shut up, cat, if you want to be fed.''

Caught between business and pleasure, Pussycat hesitated, then chose pleasure. The thing in the closet could wait. Tail indignantly erect, he followed Linda into his kitchen.

Mrs. Thomas retreated to make coffee. Will walked behind her with the boxes, which he carefully placed on a chair inside her door then went back across the foyer and called, ''Linda!''

''In here.''

He found her tearing open a packet of cat food while Pussycat told her in heart-rending tones about his deprived morning.

''There,'' she said, straightening and tucking in the back tails of her shirt. Below her the ratty tom crouched, tail switching, and began to eat ravenously.

From the kitchen door, Will said, ''I'm a dog man, myself. And a loudmouth,'' he added quietly as she turned to look at him. ''I'm sorry about this morning, Linda. I apologize.''

For what? Linda wondered. That was an unclassified apology if she'd ever heard one. General boorishness? Anger at her aerobatics? Selling her his airplane? She wanted to know about *that*, too. Yet, looking at him, the slope of big shoulders inside that blue shirt with the sleeves half-rolled on browned arms, the smear of mud on one knee, the level glance of gray eyes beneath his greasy farmer's cap—looking at all that, she felt her anger drown in a senseless tide of wanting. The warm rush of defenseless longing made her voice sound choked: "It's all right."

"No. No, it's not."

There was a detached part of him appalled at his determined self-destruction. She'd accepted his apology; he'd done his part and handsomely, too, so he ought to quit while he was ahead.

He couldn't. He had to bite the sore tooth some more. "You just—scared the hell out of me. I probably couldn't have landed half as well."

For a long moment she studied his face. Then at her feet, Pussycat provided a fortunate distraction. "Rowr!" he announced, indicating he was ready for seconds.

"You're a pig," she told the cat, and tore open another packet. As he launched into it with very uncatlike smacking noises, she again looked at Will and asked with studied casualness, "Would you fly with me sometime?"

She knew she'd said the wrong thing. Instantly. But like a little girl sopping up a spill, she went on in a rush, hating herself, hating him, and making everything worse. "She does something funny—or I do—at the top of a hammerhead stall. I seem to let her fall away too fast. . . ." She stopped, seeing the damage. Will's face had turned to stone, and he was gritting his teeth. "But I guess I'll work it out," she finished, feeling as lame as she sounded.

"I guess you will." His voice was as grim as his face. They continued to stare at each other, appalled at the tension between them, both wanting to repair the damage and neither knowing how.

Behind Will the foyer door opened and a voice called, "Hey, Westerson, the scales are working and you're third up!"

"Be right there," he called over his shoulder, then looked back at Linda. His heart wrenched in his chest. He couldn't cut it off; there had to be a thread left, something to pull her back to him again. He said, "Let me know about Sue. I'm in the bean field until dark, but I should be home about eight."

She took hold of the thread. She couldn't let him go. Not entirely. "All right," she said.

He forgot his pink glass and had to go back to Mrs. Thomas's for it. But she'd already closed the Bellams' door. On him? Probably. He really couldn't blame her. He cursed the bright, sunshiny day, scuffing through the scarlet leaves that blew before him down the alley to his truck.

Johnny Clemson was standing by the tailgate of his old International, also cursing. "Got a slit in the bottom of the hopper," he said as Will came up. "Just a little slit, but I bet I lost enough beans to fill a bin. What y' got—something for your girlfriend?"

But Will's mind had suddenly gone "click"!

Slit! That was it. That was the guy. Slit. Hauled in a dozen times on a dozen charges, but none of them ever stuck. What the hell was he doing in this little town?

"Yeah," he said briefly about the girlfriend, and put the box lid carefully on the worn truck seat. The boys at the sheriff's office had been moaning last week about nothing to do with their new equipment. Well, here was their chance. Ten nice fingerprints from a big-city hood who'd so far kept himself squeaky clean.

If it was Slit.

And, if it was, his presence in Penfield gave Will a genuine shiver. He'd seen the eyes behind the dark shades; they were as friendly as a cobra.

"Next!" whistled the guy on the scales, and Will started up his truck to follow the leaky International.

What the hell did he think he was doing? He wasn't a cop anymore; he was a farmer, and he still had sixty acres of beans to combine before nightfall.

Still—it couldn't hurt to find out . . .

In the dark closet, Slit stood silently, patiently. The blood was drying on his hand, bonding flesh to glove, and his leg and chest still stung. But those were small things, and at the moment unimportant.

She was still in the apartment. His keen ears had heard everyone else leave, and she was there. Alone.

Things were working his way, now.

Chapter Five

STRANGE HOW THE empty apartment echoed. Except for the scratching and smacking of the large fat cat at her feet, there was nothing to make noise, yet sound was there.

Perhaps it was just Will Westerson's footsteps marching off the porch, scuffing through the dry leaves—or the slowing thump of her own heart, tight with hurt, torn with indecision.

But sounds there were, real or imaginary, and she didn't care for them. Linda glanced around the messy kitchen and felt pure envy for Sue Bellam.. Sue had Ron's love and would soon have, if it wasn't here already, a baby they both wanted. The highest goals in the Bellam book were a promotion for Ron and money to buy their own house. Such a simple life.

How had she let her own get so complicated?

She turned, scraped the congealed bacon and overcooked eggs down the disposal; the harsh growl of its motor was good background music for her bitter musings.

It wasn't as though she'd never been in love before, though it hadn't been many times. She'd thought she was in love with Tim—handsome, dashing Tim, who'd worked for her dad and had been her instructor for her instrument rating. And a few other things. When he dumped her for a blond who sold Avon, she'd thought she'd surely die. But that was ten years ago. Now she could laugh about Tim.

She could not laugh about Will.

Maybe in ten more years. . . .

Then, of course, there was Tony. Also a pilot, and even more dashing and handsome than Tim. She'd married him in a fine, unthinking blaze of passion and it had become obvious all too soon that she'd made a big mistake. Tony knew a great deal about making love but nothing about loving. All the same, at this distance, Linda wished him well. Particularly as long as he stayed that way—at a distance.

They were still friends. That was fashionable. He called her occasionally from St. Louis and seemed genuinely sorry that she'd moved away. Penfield, she thought, uncharitably, was too far to be convenient when he needed a button sewed on, a homecooked meal, or a shoulder to cry on when his numerous girlfriends failed him.

But that was Tony. Women had always fallen all over themselves to take care of him, he thought it was his due. And perhaps that, also, was the reason she was so attracted to Will. He was everything Tony was not—quiet, solitary, reliable, banked fire.

Her tears joined the mess in the disposal.

At her feet, Pussycat was carefully grooming himself, one hind leg hoisted like a furry banner and his rough tongue worrying a recalcitrant spot of tar. He had not, however, lost track of the unfinished business in his life.

As Linda turned off the disposal he lowered the leg and left the tar for later licking. There was still an enemy in the bedroom closet. He rubbed his plush flank against Linda's ankle, looked up at her with enormous green eyes.

"Is that a 'thank you'?" asked Linda. "If so, you're welcome."

"Miaou!" replied Pussycat sharply. He darted toward the inner door, his plume of a tail erect as a flag. He stopped, looked back, and said, "Miaou!" again.

Linda sighed. "If you want out, PC, use your pet door. You know you're not allowed in the foyer."

The big tom came back inside twelve inches, stared at her piercingly, then wheeled and darted toward Sue's bedroom. He went out of sight, but his voice came back harshly, "Miaou! MIAOU!"

Now what? Linda sighed again. Every time she was around

Pussycat, her own desire for a pet to keep her company diminished another notch. She put the skillet and the saucepan in the dishwasher and slammed the door. She supposed she'd better see what the silly cat was up to in there.

She found him parading back and forth before the closet door, his eyes narrowed and his tail lashing furiously. As she entered, he stopped, sniffed at the louvered door, hissed, and looked back at her again, his whiskers stiff with fury. "Rowrrrr!" he said, a sort of war cry that started deep in his throat and belled to a hoarse shout of anger.

A mouse. Of course. The nights were growing cool, the mice were moving inside in droves, and he had one cornered in the clothes closet. Linda had no affection for mice, but she'd seen Pussycat in action before, and her feelings were totally with the other team. Ron could deal with the cat-versus-rodent problem. Not her.

"Forget it, Buster," she replied rudely. However, since she was there, it would be a kindness to make up Sue's bed.

She shoved the enormous old rocking chair against the closet door so she could walk all around the four-poster. Pussycat immediately hopped up on the seat, stretched to his fullest height and thrust his forepaw angrily in slashing darts through the louvers.

Golly, Linda thought laughing, *if the mouse is that tall, cat, you couldn't pay me to open the door for you!*

The opposite sheet corner was snagged on something. She edged by the rocker, went to the other side of the bed, and saw the problem. Some way—possibly during the morning's excitement—Sue's prized fluffy-ruffle begonia plant had been knocked off the bed table. It lay broken on the trailing sheet, with soil and peat moss and water making a large wet mess on the carpet.

Linda sighed, righted the pot, and shoved at the bed manfully, pushing it against the rocking chair. She couldn't save the shattered plant, but she could clean up the dirt and most of the water.

It took a bunch of paper towels, but at last she pronounced the spot dry enough. She plucked off the sheet and put on another from the hall shelf. It didn't match, but her lunch hour was going too fast to worry about aesthetics. Then, readjusting the spread on that side, she moved around to the other, grunting inelegantly as she shoved the heavy bed back to its proper spot.

"Okay, Pussycat. Get down. Get down, darn it!"

His reply was to crouch on the rocking chair seat and fizz through the back slats like a leaky hoseline. His tail lashed.

Linda sighed, but with no time to argue, she tugged both cat and solid old chair away from the closet and put it back beside the tidy bed. The cat sprang to the floor, raised up on his hind legs, and unleashed a torrent of misunderstood and abused cat sounds.

Linda muttered, "Oh, for Pete's sake! All right! All right, you ridiculous brat! Move back, and I'll open it for you!"

Inside the door, Slit drew a soundless breath. He was half-smiling. It looked as if he'd make it home tonight after all.

Linda put her hand on the knob. Pussycat went into hysterics. Slit's lethal hands tightened, ready.

The phone rang in the living room.

Linda responded to the sound like a racehorse at the starting gate.

Lips drawn back over his teeth in savage disappointment, he watched her go, leaving that insane feline to huff up and down before the door like a small volcano.

And I'll get you, too, you damned furball, he promised in silent hatred, *you're second on my list.*

He strained his ears to hear as the broad picked up the telephone. He heard her sputter, "What? When? How's Sue? What is it? Oh, Ron, I'm so excited. I'll be right there!"

Cat or not, she mustn't get away from him this time! He figured it swiftly—three long fast strides, a hand over her mouth, and she was his.

Then he'd kick the hell out of that cat.

One gloved hand closed on the inside knob. He cracked it. Big muscles bunched for the silent leap.

It didn't come off.

On the split second, a new female voice called from the living room doorway, "Coffee's ready." And the furious cat, catching one glimpse of his enemy, hurled himself.

The closet door shut. The spitting projectile thumped, rolled, and gave a screech of baffled fury. In the living room, Linda was dancing little Mrs. Thomas around, impervious to the cat noises. She was caroling, "It's a girl, it's a girl, Sue's fine, and Ron says I can see her—do you want to go?"

"Oh, my dear, I am so glad, but I can't. Ben will be home shortly. What is the matter with that cat?"

"Nothing. He's just being his usual spoiled self—and I think he has a mouse cornered in the closet."

"From the noise it must be a kangaroo! Did Will leave?"

"Yes." No elaborations. Linda looked about for her jacket, realized she'd left it in the car, dialed her office, asking as she waited for Vivian to answer, "Sure you can't come with me?"

"Quite sure. Give Sue our love."

"Oh, I will. Viv. Linda. I'm going to be late. Sue had her baby. Cover for me?"

In the stuffy closet, Slit was straining his ears, cursing the maddened tomcat hissing at him through the louvered door like a malevolent lynx. *Just you wait, bucko,* he promised, *when I come out, this coat is coming ahead of me; you're going to find yourself rolled up and stomped!*

The old lady had come into his line of sight. She was saying, "Linda, if you like, I'll take charge of Pussycat. Then no one will have to worry."

"Oh, Mrs. Thomas, would you? I'd so appreciate it. Come here, Pussycat. Hey, you! Fur Mop!"

Pussycat turned his head momentarily. Into that small pause Mrs. Thomas said in a distinct voice, "Salmon."

Pussycat hesitated.

"Salmon," she said again, and snapped her fingers. She

didn't confuse the issue with excess conversation. It wasn't necessary.

Pussycat weighed his priorities. The closet door would be there forever, but salmon was a very ephemeral thing.

He gave a last hiss, which said, in effect, I'll tend to you later, you may be sure of that! Then he trotted past Mrs. Thomas and sat down in her open doorway, making a prut-prut-prut noise in his throat.

Both the women laughed.

"You fraud," Linda said, and gave his velvet back a stroke in passing. "Okay. I'll run to the hospital. Thanks, Mrs. Thomas."

The apartment door closed behind all of them.

Gritting his teeth with baffled frustration, Slit slipped out of the closet. He caught a sudden, ghostly glimpse of himself in the bureau mirror. The disheveled, sweaty man with brown lines of blood streaking his shirt and pants leg not only dismayed him but it hurt his pride. Slit worked with neatness and dispatch; his whole reputation was involved here. Maybe he wouldn't just waste this broad and go. Maybe he was entitled to a little fun. Maybe she ought to pay for running him all over this rube town. . . .

So she was going to the hospital because some other broad had had a baby. All right. He'd find her. But first he'd better take care of himself. That gash on his hand was ragged and it hurt.

He went silently into the bathroom and worked swiftly. A bare three minutes later, hair smoothed, jacket zipped over the tears in his shirt, he gave himself a close but satisfied scrutiny. Okay. The small bulk that was Joey's money pouch was hardly detectable. He looked like any other small-town dude, God forbid! Putting the dark glasses back into place, he slipped out through the silent foyer, sauntered casually around the corner of the old white house, got in his car, and drove away. No one paid the slightest attention.

Certainly no one noticed that the tongue was working the

thin lips again. Hospitals, he thought, are handy places where strangers go in and out constantly. Besides, people died in hospitals all the time. No one could accuse him of being inconsiderate. The stiff arrived there eventually, anyway. He was just saving the police a trip.

Heart, that's what he was—all heart.

Chapter Six

WILL STOPPED HIS empty grain truck in front of the ancient-brick sheriff's office, got out. Feeling a bit of a fool, but determined, he opened the door and went inside.

A deputy in shirtsleeves with tie awry sat at the desk on the other side of the counter. He looked up and blinked.

"Good God!" he said. "You must have built-in antenna! They just found him!"

Will placed the lid with the glass dish gingerly on the counter top. "Not me," he said. "Coincidence. I turned my antenna in with my badge. Found who?"

"Some jaybird face down in a cow pasture. Deader 'n nit. A deer hunter almost stepped on him. That's a real pretty pink, Westerson, but I don't think the boss is the type."

"Shot? Don't touch it." Will's face had suddenly felt set in plaster.

The deputy pulled his hand away. He grinned. "Evidence, huh? Somebody clean you out of grape jelly?"

Will laughed too, but wouldn't let go. "Was he shot?"

"No. He may have choked to death; there was a piece of chewed caramel on the grass under his mouth. Did I say something right or wrong?"

"I'm not sure. Maybe neither. But I may have a connection."

"With that?" The deputy was pointing at the pink glass and looking a tad incredulous.

Doggedly, Will answered, "With that. It's probably a long shot, but run the prints on it, will you?"

"Sure. Want to stick around?"

"No, thanks. I've got beans in the field. But—" he hesitated, beginning to feel just a bit of an ass and hating it, "—I saw this guy in town this morning. He's got no business here, unless—"

"Unless there's something up."

"Yeah. Did they look for a knife wound—a nice, neat one?"

"I don't know. The coroner's got him now. Would a knife wound help?"

"It might. Or a broken neck."

The deputy shrugged. "All I know is he fell on his face, post mortem lividity had set in, and he had no identifying papers." He almost touched the pink glass but drew back his hand. "You think maybe these prints might ring a bell?"

If they don't, Will thought ruefully, *I am sure going to look like a big city cop throwing his weight around for nothing . . .* He answered awkwardly, "It's a long, long shot—almost so long as to be nonexistent. But damn it. On the premise that it is the same guy, what worries me is why he's still in town. His method is not to hang around."

They looked at each other. Will suddenly felt very *old* and very much in the way. He went on, "Anyway, check it out. Who knows? I'd appreciate hearing what you find."

"Sure. Sure thing. Where was this yard sale?"

"Fayette. Behind the scales."

"Okay. We'll get on it."

And as Will turned to go out, he heard the deputy add, "Thank you, sir."

It was the "sir" that really whitened his beard. As he climbed into his truck he wondered ruefully if he had ever been young like that.

Ten years ago, buddy. Just ten years ago.

"Hey! Will!" It was the deputy, standing in the doorway.

Will stuck his head out, "Yeah?"

"Will you be seeing Linda Pietra?"

The question took him by surprise, "I might. Why?"

"Tell her they found her glasses."

He didn't think to ask who; he just nodded, waved his hand, and drove off.

He did, however, leave town by way of Fayette Street and with a sinking feeling saw that the old Ford was gone. Why a sinking feeling? It was probably good news; if that was the character he thought it was, his absence was greatly to be desired.

Still, the ex-cop in him argued, the car being gone didn't necessarily mean he was gone, too, just that he'd moved elsewhere.

So what? It was out of his hands, not his affair, none of his business. Or so he lectured himself all the way back to the farm. Anyway, it probably hadn't been the same guy at all; he'd made an ass of himself at the sheriff's office and was also out seven bucks. And still he had all those beans to combine.

The hospital clock said twelve-forty-five as he drove by. On lawn chairs beneath the stately maples, three white-capped nurses were brown-bagging it, and those same maples prevented his noticing a tall, muscular gentleman in dark glasses taking a casual stroll across the crowded parking lot.

Slit's own car was parked on the north street, headed outward. Linda's dark blue Chevy hadn't been hard to spot. He paused by it, putting a large foot on the bumper to tie a shoelace. The car was unlocked, of course. Under lowered lids his eyes missed nothing. There was the camera on the back seat. He glanced around as casually as a man just getting his bearings. No one was watching. One long arm reached in, picked up the camera.

The first shock was finding it empty. The second was hearing a small voice ask, "Wanna take my picture, mister?"

He looked down. In the general area of his kneecap was an animated Charlie Daniels western hat with arms and legs. With considerable restraint, Slit said, "Go find your mommy, little kid."

The hat slipped back far enough to reveal two blue eyes, a button nose, and a milk moustache. ''Take my picture and I will.''

Slit raised the camera and clicked an empty shutter. ''There. Now beat it.''

The blue eyes didn't even blink. ''Nuffin comed out.''

''It's not the coming-out kind.''

''That's a dumb camera.''

Slit took a careful breath. ''Look, kid, I'm busy. You run off and play.''

''Gimme a quarter and I'll go.''

Slit fished in his pocket and found a half dollar. ''Here. It'll go twice as far.''

The urchin took the coin, settled his hat on his ears, and ran. At the corner of the hospital he turned, yelled back derisively, ''Yah! Dumb ol' guy! I would have taken a dime!''

But Slit was staring at the empty camera as if by sheer mental force he could elicit answers. Where was the damned film? Had she handed it over to the cops? He was feeling a positive chill for the first time in quite a few years. When had he had such rotten, lousy luck!

Suddenly, from the corner of his eye he saw her—the broad. She was coming out of the west door of the hospital and that damned state trooper was with her!

In one smooth movement he dropped the camera back on the seat and sauntered on down the row of parked cars. Near the end he found a van that offered both concealment and a side mirror that could be focused on the blue Chevy.

He couldn't, however, hear the conversation in which Ron Bellam said proudly, ''Damn! Now I guess I've got to go buy cigars.''

Linda stood on tiptoe, kissed his cheek. ''Congratulations, Dad. I guess you'd better. Hey, where do you go for cigars? The drugstore?''

''Yeah.''

''Drop off a roll of film for me? If I go I'll be late.''

"Sure. Glad to do it."

In baffled fury, Slit watched Linda Pietra reach into the pocket of the brown jacket laid over her car seat, take out a roll of film, and give it to the trooper. Jeez! The jacket! More lousy luck!

She got in her car and backed out.

The trooper's car was in the next row. The trooper tossed the roll of film up on the dash, started his engine, and drove away.

Slit stood for a moment, then made a quick decision. He could always find the broad; he knew where she lived. But he had to get hold of that film!

He got into his Ford and followed the trooper.

Naturally, straight as a die, the trooper drove four blocks east, hung a left, and parked at the sheriff's office. Of course. What else?

But he left the roll of film on the dash of the car.

Contemptuously, Slit's lip curled. Stupid upstate hick cop. When brains were passed out he'd sure been in the john. On the other hand, how do you rip off a cop car parked in front of the sheriff's office with three guys sitting right inside the window?

Worrying his lower lip, he surveyed the premises. There was a double row of retail stores lining the street, and the parking slots were filled on either side of him . . . Quite a stir of traffic as the local yokels tried to get back to work before the clock struck one . . . a fat guy stood on the corner picking his teeth and carrying a sample case in the other hand; as the church bell bonged the hour, he straightened his vest and went into the Western Auto store . . .

Another guy was coming up the block sticking flyers under windshield wipers; as he got closer, Slit could see he was about sixteen and under the curly black hair his eyes were the wide, blank eyes of innocence. About half a bubble off.

Bingo.

The boy reached out an arm to lift the Ford's wiper. Slit said genially, "Hey, kid," and slid his long legs out of the car.

The kid looked scared. He stuttered, "They pay me to do this, mister."

"Yeah, I know. I know they do. But you look tired. Here, let me finish this street and you go get a soda."

The kid hesitated, but his fingers closed over the dollar bill. "You'll do the street? I don't want 'em mad at me."

"Sure I will. I promise."

"Okay. Thanks, mister, you're a neat dude."

He shoved his bright yellow sheaf into Slit's hands and sprinted off.

Slit reached into the back seat for Joey's old ballcap, tugged it over his eyes, put his dark glasses in his shirt pocket, and started casually down the row of cars, sticking flyers under the wipers. He never even looked in the direction of the sheriff's office.

Reaching in for the film was a snap. The roll went quickly into a pants pocket. True to his promise, he stuck flyers all the way down the block, then doubled back through the alley to his Ford, tossed the cap on the seat with the account books again, replaced his dark glasses, and started the car.

With the film in his pocket, his mind was easy once more. His *forte* was, after all, simply wasting designated people. He didn't like coping with complications. Now he was back to Square One: Get the broad.

In this hick town it should be a piece of cake. Even if she hadn't gone home, he knew how to find her. As long as that little airplane sat there, she would be around. And there was always some dumb cluck to tell him where. In the meantime, he'd better find a pay phone and order flowers for his wife. He never wanted to disappoint Mona.

Of course, with those diamond earrings this job of dispatching Joey was going to pay for, she'd hardly be disappointed long. . . .

Chapter Seven

WILL WOULD HAVE felt a good deal better about his trip to the sheriff's office had he known that later that afternoon the fingerprints from his cute candy jar were affording his old friend Lieutenant Elman a great deal of pleasure. Of the three people in the shabby precinct office, Elman may not have needed cheering the most, but it was nevertheless welcome.

The second occupant was Will's sometime girlfriend, Doris Murphy. Doris, now that she knew for certain she was pregnant, was in a vile humor. Elman, who had been quietly and patiently in love with her for more than a year, was feeling the patience part sorely tried. Steve Staszewsky, the third member of the conference and the precinct lothario, had just caused Doris to explode again.

All he'd done was make one of his customary routine overtures, to which she usually responded with a wisecrack. Today she handed him his head. Not that it discouraged Steve. He was too vain to discourage. But chiefly, he was too excited to care. He could laugh now about losing Westerson's lieutenancy to Elman the Plodder. Who needed it? Steve Staszewsky was smart enough to play both sides of the cop business and get away with it and smart enough to appreciate an opportunity when he saw one. And this one was the best he'd ever seen.

The shadow known as "Slit" had just become one of the walking dead. He'd finally screwed up an assignment. One two-bit bookie and prints on a candy jar had done him in.

Steve hadn't hurried to Slit's employer with the news. He'd thought about it first, fully and carefully. If handled correctly it could have a glorious two-pronged effect, and he wanted both prongs. First, he was the logical one to take the contract for removing Slit with its gratifying monetary compensation. Second, removal would leave a vacancy, which Steve had waited a long time to fill.

Slit had done very well for himself—but who was he? Nothing but a musclebound schnook with quick reflexes.

Steve could do better. A lot better.

Smarts. That's what it took: plain old all-American smarts!

The tense silence in the office following Doris's outburst failed to faze Steve, who smiled across the desk at Elman.

Elman did not smile back, but Steve never noticed. Nor did he realize that Elman hadn't smiled at him for quite some time. In Steve's book he was everybody's darling. He pressed on cheerfully, "So ol' Slit has been spotted in Pike County just when they found a body! Isn't that a coincidence!"

Elman replied, "Mff." He was running his eye down the report just handed in.

Undaunted, Steve went on, "And Pike is pretty sure they'll pick him up. I'm off duty today and tomorrow. Shall I pop up there for you and bring baby home?"

With enormous difficulty John Elman kept his eyes on the report sheet. He was thinking angrily, *Wouldn't you love that, wouldn't it hand the man to you on a plate! Then what? A sad accident? Gee, I'm sorry, chief, the gun just went off! Or something more dramatic than that—a battle to the death, a ripped suit, bruises maybe. But not, of course, on your face. You'd never damage your face, would you, Apollo? You make me gag. Wouldn't that surprise you!* Aloud, he said, "They haven't got him yet."

Steve almost offered to go and assist but thought better of it. It might look too eager, too suspicious. He'd just go anyway. Without Elman's say-so. It was too good a chance to miss—and besides, when the newspapers got hold of his wiping a piece of scum off the face of the earth, hero stuff like that would make it pretty hard for Elman to complain about disobeying orders. There were so many ways of handling Dullsville cops like Elman . . .

The lieutenant was looking at Doris. "Who's on the duty roster if we need him?"

"I'll go check."

She left. Steve said, "Cheerful as a tomb, isn't she?"

"She's tired. She's been working overtime." It was more than that, and John knew it, but he also felt that Dorrie's problems were damned well none of Staszewsky's business.

Steve looked at his watch—a three-hundred-dollar affair with all the fancy gadgets. Elman, he noticed, wore a Timex. "I have an appointment," he said. "I'll call in about five to see what's going on."

He left behind a trail of Pierre Cardin. Elman got up and opened a window, but not strictly for ventilation. After a moment or so, he saw Steve leave in his silver Corvette. He also saw one of his boys fall in behind. Good. Great. Things were moving.

He didn't know which would give him more pleasure: removing a cold reptile like Slit, or a rogue cop like Staszewsky. At the moment he'd almost opt for saving the reptile. Snakes, after all, were pretty much loners. A bad policeman usually had more tentacles than an octopus.

Doris came back and put a list before him. She was smiling, but there were deep violet lines beneath her eyes.

He took a deep breath and asked quietly, "Dorrie, can I help? Whatever it is. If you have a money problem—"

She shook her head with its fluffy crown of well-maintained red-brown hair. "No money problem. Exactly. It's just—personal. I'll work it out. Thanks, anyway, John."

Lieutenant Elman was no Will Westerson, but he was nice. His wife had been dead three years; he was finally losing that haunted look. Selling his house and moving out of the county had probably helped. You shouldn't live in the past, her mother always said. The past was certainly not her problem. Not now.

The sergeant brought Elman a carton of coffee and a cheeseburger. Doris sat down and began to type. He finished the cheeseburger, balled up the paper, and reached into his desk for the Rolaid bottle. Smiling slightly, she said, ''Already? You just ate!''

''Preventive medicine. It's not the cheeseburger, though. I made spaghetti for dinner last night and I don't think I've quite got the hang of it, yet.''

''I do pretty good spaghetti—for an Irish girl. I'll make it for you, sometime.''

His breath caught. Be casual, Elman. Very casual. ''I'd like that. Say when.''

And suddenly Doris found herself thinking, *No, I'm not ready for this—I'm not ready for anything new—especially with John, who could get awfully hurt. I have to decide some things first.* She turned away, put her cover on her typewriter. ''Sure. Next week, maybe. Anyway, this starts my forty-eight. So I'll see you Tuesday.''

''Get some sleep. You could use it. Take care of yourself, Dorrie.''

''Oh, I do,'' she replied wearily. ''Really well.''

She went home, turned on the four o'clock soap opera, turned it off again, and sat staring at the wall of her apartment. A baby. An honest-to-God kid.

Her airline pilot would be sorry—she knew that. She also knew what he'd expect her to do about it. Tony Pietra had bugged out of one marriage and he was not about to bug into another one. And as far as Tony was concerned, Doris couldn't care less.

That was not the nitty-gritty.

The nitty-gritty was that she didn't want to do anything about it. The nitty-gritty was that she wanted this baby.

The hell with Tony. He could kiss off as far as she was concerned. But the tiny little person beneath the band of her Bend-Over Levis was hers. She was going to keep it.

And suddenly—blindingly—she knew how!

As Will turned into the south field, he saw the red Trans Am in his driveway. Surprised, he parked the truck and told his hired hand, "I'll be right back."

Keith nodded, shoving his tractor cap to the back of his curly head. "No hurry. I'll just have me a chew. Looks like you got company."

Will nodded. The brown bean stubble cracked under his feet as he went to the fence, climbed the gate, and dropped down, watching where he put his boots when he landed. His six purebred Charolais calves were frisky and cute but had only rudimentary ideas about sanitation. The second gate creaked as he went through it, strode briskly up the walk, moved old Bowser gently aside on the sun-warmed step, and entered the kitchen of his elderly farmhouse. He could smell fresh coffee but saw no one. "Hi!" he called cheerfully.

No answer.

The dining room with its old oak sideboard and square table was empty, too. But the living room was occupied. A half cup of coffee sat on the end table by the lamp, and Doris was asleep on the ancient sofa.

One arm pillowed her head, her soft brown hair strayed across the upper cheek. The half-unbuttoned checkered shirt was pulled from her Levis by the twist of rounded hips, and it was also unbuttoned quite a ways. The view was magnificent.

He sat beside her, brushed back the hair, and lightly kissed the cheek. "Hey. Sleepyhead." Her eyes opened languidly. But they were too clear. Will had the sudden feeling that she'd not been asleep at all. His mind went immediately on alert.

"Will . . . ," she murmured, and taking his hand from her hair, she drew his fingertips lightly across the warm curves of her breasts.

He took the hand away.

"Whoa, sweetie," he said. "I'm a working man right now. What are you doing here?"

She stretched like a kitten. "I took some days off."

"In the middle of the week?"

"Does it matter? Haven't you missed me?"

Her own hand had traveled up his tanned throat, then slipped inside his shirt to trace his collarbone. He retrieved that hand too, slapped it lightly.

"You're coming on too fast, kid," he said. "What's your problem?"

Then she laughed, swung her legs to the floor, and sat up.

"I've been deprived," she grinned. "Can't you tell?"

"I didn't notice any difference. Besides, I thought your airplane jockey was taking care of business."

"He's on a flight. Anyway, I like variety. But I can wait. There's fresh coffee."

He stood up. "It's going to be quite a wait. We won't get out of the bean field until dark tonight."

"Then I'll fix your dinner. And a few other things."

She reached for him again, but he gently held her arms against her sides. "I said I was a working man right now. I'll be back about eight."

As he crunched across the bean field toward the combine he cursed himself under his breath. Why hadn't he been able to just tell her . . . how could he tell her he didn't want her here? Didn't want her, period. He guessed he felt sorry for her. She was such a good kid, and they had had some good times, but the whole affair had been dying for almost a year. It was over now; his body told him that. It wasn't that he felt nothing at all for her—somehow, he guessed he'd been thinking of her, when he thought of her at all, as more of a *friend*. Clearly, her thoughts were not so platonic.

He had to get her out of here, and he hoped he could do it without hurting her feelings, but she had to go. Back to the city. Where she belonged.

Where he didn't belong. Not anymore. He began to wonder what he would have done had it been Linda he'd found on the couch, and his knees went weak on the outer fringes of the fantasy. He cursed again.

From the combine cab, Keith leaned out and yelled over the roar of the engine, "That was fast!"

"I'm a fast mover."

"Think you could teach me?"

"From what I hear, you don't need teaching. And anyway, it isn't speed that impressed the ladies."

The kid grinned and put the big red Massey in gear. Harvest was on again.

It didn't bother Slit to use Joey's telephone credit card; Joey obviously wouldn't need it anymore. What did bother him was that after he'd ordered the roses, he called home and Mona didn't answer.

He stood by the metal blue-and-white telephone hood mounted to the side of a Conoco station and frowned. Warm sun and playful breezes were lost on him. The scrawled graffiti never even teased the narrowed eyes behind the implacable black glasses.

The trouble was that it had happened before. Too often before. Mona laughed, said he was being ridiculous, that she'd been downtown shopping with Marcia. Marcia, of course, always backed her up.

After the one time he asked, "What did you buy?" she changed her tune and introduced a string of variations. One was that she'd had the Porsche in the shop. Then he'd come home unexpectedly one afternoon. Watching through the window, he'd seen this young stupido with bulging biceps in a muscle shirt dropping her off, all polite and proper. His name was Jerry something, she said. He worked at the body shop.

But she'd been scared; he could see it in the whites of her eyes. He told her to drop the shop and the guy fast, using a small squeeze around her throat to make the point.

But had she?

His jaw set. He used Joey's card again, dialed the body shop. He said, "Hey, is Jerry around?"

It was Jerry's day off.

There was a glow in Slit's belly like a hot coal.

Slowly, with infinite care, he twisted the telephone receiver into two pieces, laid them on the little metal shelf. Then he got back in the Ford. He put a caramel in his mouth. He chewed. He'd take care of Jerry when he got back. That was no problem.

And Mona. He'd take care of Mona, too. He'd give her the roses, he'd make love to her then he'd let her know he knew. He'd watch the fear in her eyes, listen to her try to weasel out. Maybe he'd let her think she had. For a while.

Maybe. Maybe not.

She was a pretty good mother.

But what the hell. His kids were young; they'd forget. The trouble was that he wouldn't. He'd look at her—and he'd see the other guy—what he'd done. With his woman.

Sweat broke out on Slit's face. One fist doubled. It smashed the car dash so hard it made a dent. The scratch on the back of his hand broke open and started to bleed again.

He'd worked hard to keep his other life clean of dirty fingers—the life he'd built piece by piece. He'd picked her out of a convent, a dumb little nitwit with a beautiful body; he'd married her properly. He'd bought her a house and jewels and furs and a country-club membership; he'd given her two nice kids—and this was his thanks!

Some guy in a Datsun came toward the phone. Slit drove off.

First things first. Priorities.

The yard sale was down to the rag tags, now, with a lot of empty hangers jingling on the clothes racks, all the depression glass gone and nothing left of the furniture but a moth-eaten sofa with one end held up by a brick. An old lady sat on the sofa, talking nine-to-a-dozen with another old lady. Draped across her knees like a black-and-white lap robe was Slit's old acquaintance, the tomcat.

Slit realized it was a hundred to one shot, but if he ever caught that feline alone again there wouldn't be enough left over to make a hot pad. He drove by slowly, turning his eyes behind their dark lenses toward the old white apartment house.

The broad's car wasn't there. But a state police car was. Damn. So they were giving her police protection, maybe. His lips lifted a little over his teeth. Good. He needed a challenge right now, needed to bolster his ego, shore up his own sense of worth. Let that police dude in there think he was God Almighty, Guardian of the Citizenry, Protector of the Innocent! He'd match wits with a rube state trooper anytime!

First he'd better eat. Like any predator, he preferred to be lean while hunting. But a growling stomach on a stalk could be a bit unhandy.

He wheeled through the fast-food take-out drive, ordered two double cheeseburgers and coffee, parked against the west curb, and ate them in tearing bites, washed down with tepid swigs from the plastic cup. The city cemetery, across the road, had tall old granite shafts like fingers against the coral setting sun, and a single arrogant crow perched on the highest was giving out his raucous challenge to the world. Slit saw no symbolism in this, no comparison with the poor mortality of mankind. In fact, he didn't see it at all. There was a deep fire burning inside him now, a growing restlessness, a savage griping in his very guts —but he couldn't give in. Not yet. Priorities. Priorities.

Damn all sneaking, lying, conniving women. This Linda. Probably her, too. Cheaters, all of them. She had a husband. It said so back there on the name plate—but it didn't say he was a state trooper. Who was to say she wasn't having it off right now with the fuzz while her husband, the dumb jerk, was working his tail off to make a living for her. Like him. Working his tail off, making a living for Mona while she cheated.

Mona would have to wait a while to get hers. But he'd enjoy wasting Linda. He'd probably be doing her poor jerk of a husband a favor.

So enjoy, too, Linda. While you can. Tonight your number runs out.

He wadded up the cheeseburger papers, tossed them in the rear seat. Backing out, he pointed the ratty old Ford toward Fayette Street and stopped to make one more phone call. Still no answer.

He felt as if his very blood were chilled.

The trooper car was gone from Linda's driveway. In its place was a dark Buick. A spare, erect old man with the look of command was just taking a briefcase from the trunk.

Colonel Benjamin Thomas, Retired, thought Slit. *They all look the same—like they sat on a poker.* He took off his dark glasses, put on Joey's ballcap, pulled to the curb.

"Hey, y'all," he said in a soft, slurred voice, "Where can I find Linda?"

The man hardly glanced up. "Farm Bureau office," he answered politely and told him how to find it! Incredible. What a rube town!

Slit located the office, found it to be a low brick building with a big parking lot. He parked on the back row and waited. While he sat, his thoughts went to Mona again, and they were not nice thoughts.

His insides were in a turmoil. As the afternoon darkened into the damp of early evening he began to belch cheeseburger and tried taking deep breaths to ease the heartburn. Why the hell couldn't Joey have been a mint freak instead of those damned caramels?

He wondered briefly if Joey'd been found yet. Not that it mattered. There was nothing to connect the little man with him. And he had the books and the money—dynamite for his bosses if they went into the wrong hands. But they wouldn't. Slit might work slowly but he never failed, and the big men knew it. They wouldn't worry.

All he had to do was waste the damned broad, then he was home free. As usual. No sweat.

Except for Mona.

His stomach burned, and he sat very straight to ease the hiatal hernia between his ribs. He had to do something about that, someday. When the split in his diaphragm let the top part of his stomach shove up through it, the pain was absolutely immobilizing.

Mona said they had some new procedure, now, something about using nylon net. Maybe. But he was no damned fish.

One by one the employees left, trotting across the asphalt, waving good night. Finally only three or four cars were left—among them the blue Chevy. Fine. Fine, if she worked late.

He'd been sitting two hours. He didn't care. He wasn't in a hurry, now. And he wasn't going to be in a hurry. Things would go right—the way he wanted.

Sooner or later. It didn't matter. He had the time.

Linda was as good as dead.

Chapter Eight

IN THE MIDDLE of the afternoon, the phone on Linda's office desk had rung and a cheerful voice said, "Hi!"

Linda answered, "Hi, who?" But she already knew who. Tony. Just what she needed—an ex-husband on the scene.

And being Tony, he wanted something. He went straight to the point: "Hey, I've been furloughed. How about putting me up for a few days?"

There was no point in burdening Linda with details. The situation had been made patently clear to him that morning. Until his bookie reappeared with his books and his collected money, the syndicate was making a blanket assumption that none of Joey's customers had paid. When he'd protested, one of the well-dressed bland gentlemen had said, "We'll refund."

Sure they would.

But what if they never found Joey?

Tony had paced his apartment anxiously for half an hour, cursing his lackadaisical attitude toward receipts, wondering how in billy hell he was going to come up with another forty-five hundred dollars since Deb, in Houston, had just hit him up for lease money on their little love nest down there.

Then he thought of his ex-wife.

Not that Linda had forty-five hundred dollars, but surely tight wad Linda had some of that divorce settlement money left! Besides, who would think of looking for Tony Pietra in that Podunk center where she lived? At least he could hide out for a few days.

He'd tossed some gear in a bag, gone down the service

elevator, and taken a stewardess's Datsun. She was in Switzerland; she wouldn't mind.

Now he was in a Penfield pay-phone booth. The second one. The first had its telephone receiver broken right in two—a rather repellent sight for a guy not too confident of his own welfare at the moment.

Neither had he liked the silence at Linda's end of the line. Hell, he didn't like it either! If he had more than lunch money in his pocket, he wouldn't even be in this dump! He tried his most charming voice, "Come on, Lin! No involvement. I promise. I'll even sleep on the couch."

Linda thought, *You'd better believe it, buddy.*

Acidly, she asked, "What's been slapped on you, Anthony? Breach of promise or alienation of affection?"

Okay. Let her think that. It would be just fine.

He made his charming voice humble. "Neither, but you're close. You know me too well."

"I should."

"How about it, kid? Just a few days. I'll be as good as gold. I'll warm your slippers at the fire and carry in your newspaper every night."

"I don't want you, Tony. It's not convenient."

"So you've got something else going. Okay, I'll understand. I'll be the soul of discretion. I'll be your uncle from Sioux City. I'll sit on a park bench until you wave your hanky out the bedroom window. Come *on*, Linda!"

Something different in his voice caught her ear—something genuinely anxious. She said soberly, "Tony, are you really in trouble?"

His answer was short: "Yes, Ma'am."

"I don't want any overspray, Tony."

"There won't be any overspray. I promise you."

She sighed. "All right. Until the weekend."

Bingo. "Fine. That should do it. You're a sweetheart."

"I'm a pushover. As usual. Where are you?"

''At a little quick-shop place.''

''Here?''

''Here. Didn't I say so?''

''No, you didn't say so.'' Her voice was dry. She was even more of a pigeon than she'd realized. ''Okay. Come by the office and I'll give you a key.''

''Right on!'' he answered cheerily and hung up.

So did she, and stared at the silent telephone. As though she didn't already have enough complication in her life! At least Tony didn't know about Will. He mustn't know about Will. It was, as a matter of fact, none of his damned business. Yet she knew too well that her ex-husband tended to be proprietary. It must be part of the male ego, she thought wearily, thinking of Will and the yellow Cub. What was once their's they never actually seem to surrender.

Tony showed up ten minutes later. She knew he was present before he appeared—she heard Karen's giggle in the reception room. Just a good ol' Italian boy, she told herself ruefully, and who am I to fault Karen? God knows, I fell for it, too!

A gray tweed English walking hat sailed into the office, landing on her typewriter. She sailed it back, said, ''That's not necessary. Come on in.''

He came, the hat back on his black curls, and grinned down at her impudently from his trim six feet. His smile was a naughty boy's, certain of forgiveness. He said, ''Hi.''

''Key,'' she said, and held out her hand.

He took the key, kissed the hand. She said grimly, ''Hey, remember? This is me—Linda! I don't buy that Siciliano Sunshine stuff any more.''

''Conditioned response.'' Tony was Tony; why didn't she remember also that little fazed him. ''Will Mommy be home for din?''

''Mommy doesn't know.'' Although, suddenly, she did know—and she wouldn't. ''But baby won't starve. There's ham and potato salad in the fridge. And remember, you sleep on the couch, Buster.''

"You know the damned thing is a back-breaker."

"And you know that if I find you in my bed, I'll break something else! Good-bye, Tony, I have to make a living."

"*Ciao*," he said.

"*Ciao*."

Out in the reception room Karen said it, too: "*Ciao*, Tony. Nice to see you again."

Linda puffed out her cheeks in a rueful expression of resignation and wondered what her soft heart had let her in for, once more.

Nothing, she resolved, and, setting her teeth, she went back to work.

It was a good thing. Late that afternoon, just as she got caught up, her boss came back with an armload of new Federal regulations. She was given the option of sending out for sandwiches, or waiting until everything was done, then going to dinner.

She chose the latter. What had been brewing in her head since Tony's advent came to full fruition; she was going to buy dinner at the supermarket deli, take it out to Will's farm, and tell him about Sue's baby. She'd said she would.

She could just picture him coming in, tired and dirty, smiling in pleased surprise to find her there, getting in the shower, sitting down at the table with his hair all wet, smelling of soap and water, and eating heartily while they talked and laughed. The two of them. Just the two of them.

And then? Then, she didn't know. She really didn't know. She did know what she wanted, and her heart quickened, thinking about it. *I am throwing myself at a man*, she thought, and amended the phrase, adding "again," hearing her mother's voice in the accusation.

But Mother had meant Tony Pietra, and she'd been right; her daughter had been wrong, and whatever Tony Pietra might think, there was nothing left of that marriage but some pretty shabby tatters. Tony had put her through an emotional wringer. She thought she'd learned something from it.

Surely she had. She was older now; she had a better idea of the score on the—what had Mae West called it?—the "bed-sheet battleground." At least she knew there had to be something more in a marriage than sex, or the marriage starved to death.

Linda glanced at her copy and realized she'd typed the same line of statistics three times. In dismay she ripped the pages out and rolled in a fresh one. This time she kept her traitorous mind on her work.

They finished at seven-thirty. She put the cover on her typewriter and said, "Go on. I'll lock up."

Her boss stretched and rubbed his eyes. "Okay. Thanks a lot, Lin. I'll see you in the morning. Good night."

"Good night."

She turned the key in the files, snapped off her desk lamp, and picked up her brown blazer and shoulder bag. The office door behind her clicked, and it echoed hollowly in the deep shadows of the circular lobby. There was one dim light in the hall; it silhouetted the enormous rubber tree behind Karen's desk, making the thick branches look like grasping arms. Linda shivered, even though she felt silly doing it and reproved herself. This was Penfield—little, safe Penfield, where nothing happened, ever.

There was a crack of light beneath Mr. Arlow's door, and she was almost angry at the sense of relief she felt in seeing it. She pushed the door open. The elderly maintenance man glanced up from his mopping, blinking his eyes behind thick lenses.

"Hi, Charlie," she said. "I'm going to the rest room before I leave. Don't lock me in."

"Okay. Tell me when you're ready. I'll turn on the pole light for you. The damned mercury-vapor one's burned out again."

"I will. Thank you."

The small rest room was brilliantly lighted. Its fluorescent tubes beamed mercilessly down on white tile, white lavatories, black-and-white tesselated floor, and one secretary in brown slacks and cream-colored shirt putting down her jacket and shoulder bag. The light was less than flattering and Linda's fatigue showed.

She rummaged in her purse for her makeup bag, repainted her mouth, looked at herself critically, and touched a little blusher to each cheekbone. Rats. First, she'd looked pale, now she looked like two dollars would cover everything.

Sighing, she tissued it all off and started again from scratch, ending with a fierce brushing of feathered brown hair, and wishing for the first time that she had her long, softly waving tresses back. But they'd gone long ago with marriage, as a sort of punitive backlash to everything Tony had liked.

She sighed, sucked in her stomach, and looked at herself critically. There was a new, soft, rose-colored dress hanging in her closet at home, a dress that was very flattering and even rather sexy. But she wasn't going home. Tony was there. Anyway, the rose dress would be overplaying it.

Suddenly aware of the direction of her thoughts, her blusher was glowing again. *I am mad*, she told her reflecton in the mirror. *Absolutely mad. I never knew I was such a hussy!*

I'm not. I'd better call.

He might not be in, yet. He might still be choring.

He might say no.

And I couldn't bear it. I simply couldn't bear it. And that, my dear, is that.

She picked up her jacket and bag and walked back into the lobby. It was brightly lighted now, the ceiling-high windows shining like black glass, reflecting the busy image of Charlie slopping scrub water on dark tile. He straightened, pushed his glasses up. "Ready?"

"Ready."

She left under escort, her heels clicking, into a night turned cool and damp with a muzzy moon just riding the treeline.

"Rain by morning," Charlie said conversationally. "I'll leave the light on and stand out here until you get your car started."

"Thanks. I appreciate it. See you in the morning."

She didn't know why she felt so jittery. It must be because the security lamp being out made the lot so much darker.

Her heels clicked like gunshots. Her car door creaked like a soul in pain. Feeling like an idiot, she checked the back seat, found it empty, and slid onto the clammy cushion beneath the wheel. The car started obediently. She waved to Charlie, put it in gear, and drove out into the street, shrugging into her jacket with one hand. It was cold enough to make her teeth chatter.

Linda didn't notice the car following hers into the supermarket parking lot. She walked past the piles of bright orange pumpkins and black paper cats, grateful for the heat inside the automatic doors. A very small boy in a very large cowboy hat said, "Trick or treat for UNICEF."

She paused. "Where's your can?"

"It's coming next week."

"I'll pay next week," she answered shortly. The kid only grinned. Irritated, she yanked loose a grocery cart.

As she went down the aisle, a taller boy appeared: "Trick or treat for UNICEF." He had a can. She put a dollar in it and told him, "You have competition back there."

He grimaced. "That's my bratty brother. I've chased him home twice." He took off at a trot, saying over his shoulder, "Thanks, lady."

Linda wheeled on around to the deli section, reflecting that if the boy in the Charlie Daniels hat was so adept at a rip-off at five, they'd better nail the courthouse down when he turned fifteen.

Everything looked good because she was hungry. She had them wrap up two slabs of barbecued ribs, fill one carton with beans, the other with potato salad, roll a French loaf in foil, and cut out two pieces of cheesecake. Her car had warmed up while she'd been in the store, but the glow she really felt was a beginning excitement.

As she headed out of town to Will's farm, she noticed grain trucks still lined up on the scales drive but thought little about it. By the time she was passing the airport she had her windshield wipers working steadily, clearing fanlike shapes in the sparkling mist. The dips and hollows flanking the highway with scrub cedar and slender sycamores were filled with ghostly patches of drifting fog. She might have a hard time getting back to town.

Perhaps she wouldn't have to get back. . . .

Impulsively she turned into the airport drive and parked at the gate. As she opened it, she saw the flashing beacon getting its red and green beam swallowed in gossamer. The security lights were balls of filmy nebulae. Her yellow Cub glistened with wet. As she approached, she saw Tom had been as good as his word. The wire gas gauge was standing up full high, one drop of water appending like a diamond from its top.

There was also a ''For Sale'' sign hung on the prop.

Linda suddenly felt a little sick. She wasn't sure selling the plane would help matters with Will that much and she did know she'd hate to give it up. The windows were up tight, and there was no slack in the tie-down ropes. Still, it ought to be in a hangar before winter. A fabric airplane had no business sitting outside.

Huddled in her jacket, feeling like a traitor, she headed back to the gate. She could see a row of heads inside the window of the small terminal, and Tom popped his out of the door. ''Hi. Do you really want to sell the Cub, Linda? I've had a guy ask already.''

Linda shook her head. ''I don't know,'' she answered ruefully. ''There's an air show at my dad's field next week. I'm supposed to fly in it. Maybe I'll make up my mind after that. Hi, Jim. Kent.''

The two guys who'd pushed past Tom walked with her to the parking lot, zipping their jackets against the chill. Kent opened her door for her. ''Going back to town? I'll buy coffee.''

''No. Thanks, anyway.''

Ahead of them, she pulled out onto the misty road, turned

north. As far as she could see through the drifting fog, Will's adjacent bean field was silent and shorn. Good. He'd be done, then. Maybe already in the shower . . .

She snapped on her left-turn signal, waited for the steaming, snarling red and green dragon that was an approaching eighteen-wheeler. It went by, grating and growling as the trucker geared down for the hill. Vaguely, she saw another set of lights in her rearview mirror, also moving slowly. As she turned into the narrow lane that was Will's driveway, the car went on by. Still slowly. But she paid no attention.

Will's lane went up and down like a rollercoaster, sided with fence rows full of bittersweet and jack oak, rutted by tractor wheels, and occasionally blotted out by clouds of fog. Once she heard water running and knew she was crossing the culvert over Bay Creek. And once, at the top of a slope, she thought she saw lights behind her. Strange. She'd thought this was a private drive. But perhaps it wasn't. Anyway, ahead, on the left, was the fuzzy blue light on its pole in Will's barn lot.

There were lights in the living room, too, and a dim one in the kitchen. He was home. Will was home.

As she pulled onto the level, crushed-rock parking space by the machine shed, suddenly she realized that the jouncing she'd felt for about half a mile had not been totally tractor ruts. Her left rear tire, steel-belted radial or not, was almost flat.

Damn.

Oh, well. Later.

As she gathered the grocery sacks into her arms, shifting them so as to see over the top, she was abruptly, unsettlingly aware that her heart was beating like a trip-hammer and her tongue was stuck to the roof of her mouth.

When he opened the door, what would she say?

Something cute: "Trick or treat!"

No. Not that. She could never carry it off. She was not the cute type.

Something simple: "Hi . . . Would you like something to eat?"

70

God no. That sounded as if she was selling Girl Scout cookies.

How about: "I hope you like ribs" or a plain "I've brought your dinner . . . and Bellam's had a girl."

All this time her feet were carrying her automatically across the crushed rock, through the gate, and up the cracked and weedy sidewalk.

The screen door was wet to her hand. She opened it, leaned one bag against the porch wall and knocked.

She was committed. She couldn't run away now.

Her heart was thumping so hard it almost choked her.

Feet. She could hear feet.

The knob turned. The old wooden door resisted, sticking, then opened. Linda said breathlessly, "Hi. I hope you—"

Over her the woman in the doorway was saying, "Will, why did you knock? Are you playing games. If you want—"

Then they both stopped. There was a terrible silence.

Candlelight from the dining room silhouetted the woman in the doorway. Her hair was tumbled on her shoulders. She wore a sheer black nightgown. And not too much of that.

Speechless, they stared at each other. Just one moment. An eternity. But still, just one moment.

Then the woman in the door said softly, "Oops."

Linda turned and ran.

Chapter Nine

ONE OF THE sacks burst in the wet. She stumbled, kicked it aside, wrenched open the car door, threw the other helter-skelter into the back, started the engine, and sprayed gravel in a sweeping curve as she headed out toward the driveway again. She was half-blinded with tears of humiliation, sobbing great wrenching sobs of embarrassment.

She only got about half a mile before her rear tire told her she'd forgotten about it once, but she couldn't forget about it any longer.

Just on the other side of the creek culvert she pulled drunkenly off as far as she could into the scratchy brambles, turned off her engine, laid her head on the wheel, and wept.

It didn't help.

Tears had never helped her. All they really did was smear her makeup until she looked like a kid's paint box, swell her eyes half-shut, screw up her contact lenses, and mottle her skin with ugly patches of red.

That's what they had done now. She couldn't say she felt any better for the release, and she was still all alone, stranded on a little-used country lane in the ruin and fog. The tire was still flat.

How can I ever face Will? Why didn't I have sense enough to call? Stupid, stupid, stupid!

She snuffled sternly. *You are,* she told herself, *in a bitter mood, and what's needed here is some action.* The flat had to be changed. Not a comfortable prospect—in fact, a totally miserable one—but feeling sorry for herself wouldn't get it done. She pulled on the orange flasher lights, got out onto the slick muddy grass, and opened the trunk.

The tractor ruts were filled with water. She discovered this quickly, as one high-heeled, open-toed shoe went into one up to her ankle. She shivered, bit her lip, mopped her eyes, and in the dim light of the trunk lid, surveyed the spare tire. It looked sound. It was also firmly fastened to the side of the trunk. She tugged, broke a nail jaggedly, said a word generally found on sidewalks. That black thing was the jack. But how did it work?

She lugged out two awkward pieces, looked at them in the spastic light of the flashers, realized she was a piece short, and found it.

Come on, she said to herself grimly. *This is true life, girl. You can't go back to Will's. So either you use your brains like a sensible woman or you've got a long, wet walk to civilization with the possible chance of getting mugged, raped, or run over along the highway.*

It took ten long bitter minutes in the cold and wet to figure the damned jack out, then about five more rooting around on the creek edge for a flat enough rock to put beneath it so it wouldn't sink in the mire. Just as she was climbing back over the fence something whuffled in the darkness behind her, scaring her so badly she tore her pants on the barbed wire and dropped the rock on her foot. When the opaque silhouette of a roaming cow appeared against the skyline, she didn't even find it vaguely funny to have been so needlessly frightened.

Then when the car was half jacked up, it rolled forward because she'd forgotten to block the wheels. The sidewalk word was augmented by a bus station rest-room favorite. But at least she'd learned something.

She propped her glove compartment flashlight up on a wet and rusty beer can and crouched to pry at the hubcap. It came off with a tinny rattle. A vague recollection of her father changing tires prompted her to use it as a receptacle for the bolts on the wheel.

It was raining by now—softly, insidiously. Her hair hung in strings over her eyes, her jacket was wet, greasy, and had a pocket torn down. She'd never been so cold. Her fingers were numb. She put one hand inside her blouse to warm it while she removed the last lug nut with the other hand, then went down on both knees on the harsh rock. Both arms around the wheel, grunting, panting, she lifted it off, getting mud and dirt on the few places still clean. Then she straightened and, with a feeling of triumph that ignored aching back muscles, rolled it around, hoisted it up, and flopped it into the trunk.

Now. Stage two.

Should she sit in the car a moment, get just a little warm?

It was a terrible temptation. But something told her if she did she'd crumble, she'd cave in like a piece of wet cardboard, and she'd never have the courage to get out in the cold muck again.

Besides, if she licked this thing herself, all by herself, it wouldn't make her feel less a fool about Will, but at least she'd know she could do something right!

Grimly, she got her flashlight, tackled the spare in its snug groove. It cost her another nail and maybe a hernia, but she tumbled it down to the road, rolled it around, repositioned the flashlight, and tried to lift it up to fit on the hub.

She simply couldn't quite get it high enough.

She almost cried. Damn it. The hard part was supposed to be done!

She took her flashlight and straightened up, throwing the beam around her into the wet and tangled underbrush, the fence row, the roadbed, searching for inspiration. There had to be a way . . . Then she remembered.

There was a way. If it worked. It had to work.

She leaned the wheel gingerly against the car and went back to the trunk. There was a big carton of outdated government pamphlets on herbicides that she'd saved for Sue to line PC's litterbox. Sorry, PC.

Hefting the carton, she trudged back to the tire, knelt, put an inch-thick stack down on the mud, rolled the big wheel half on it, steadied the tire with her shoulder, pushed another stack beneath the tire and on top of the first stack, then another and another. It took almost all of the carton, but finally, thanks to the United States Agricultural Service, the wheel was finally high enough so she could lift it on.

"Yea," she applauded herself, spatting her muddy hands together like a perfect fool. Totally abandoning cleanliness to comfort, this time she sat on the wet roadbed, as she put the hardware back on, tightening the bolts fiercely and wiping the rain running down into her eyes with whatever muddy hand was free.

The last thing was letting down the jack.

She held her breath.

The tire stayed round. There was air in it.

The sense of accomplishment that swept her was almost primitive. She threw the jack, the muddy Ag bulletins, and the hubcap in the back, slammed down the trunk lid, and with simple, unreasoned exhilaration so exquisite as to be almost drunken, she did a ridiculous, hilarious, muddy dance right in the middle of the road.

The flashlight was still in her hand. It described arcs and beams across the water-laden, weed-grown roadbanks as she jigged, inscribing a sort of fairy polka of its own.

Then it caught the dark, wet outline of a man standing on the bank. Staring down at her.

The beam froze. A spotlight.

Simple terror bubbled in her throat, turned to a scream. The flashlight fell from her nerveless hand, rolled away, and mirrored nothing further but crushed pigweed in a ditch. But it didn't matter, nothing mattered, because she'd seen him, and the crashing in the wet brush of the bank told her he was coming!

She dived for her car, jamming down the door locks, sobbing hysterically as she tried to turn the ignition key with numb, wet fingers. The engine started, died. The dark mass seemed to be moving now, toward the car. The Chevy roared. She jammed it into gear, shot into the roadbed spraying mud and water, scraped the bank on the other side, straightened out, plunged down the slope toward the black pit of the culvert across the creek, got two wheels off the track, plowed about twenty feet into soft turf, and came to a grinding, useless halt.

Back at the top of the slope, Slit made an almost animal sound of satisfaction as he heard the sound. Stuck.

Very good.

Wiping the muddy spray from his face, he started down the wet ruts, slipping a little, feeling the cold mist against his already sodden body, but moving in. Inexorably moving in.

He was out of his element. He knew it. He'd sat a long time in the car parked along the highway, debating about the dark lane, fearing a cul-de-sac—and hating the wet as a big cat hates it. But she'd gone down that narrow wagon track, and she hadn't come back. It had been worth a shot.

He'd watched as she'd struggled with the tire, letting her change it. Better her than him. He had no desire to walk back to the other car. That she'd seen him was unfortunate. But, now that she was stuck, it didn't really matter.

Even on the rutted surface of the road he walked lithely. Water dripped from the bill of the ballcap and his wet cheekbones felt frozen. But his hands were warm inside the slash pockets of his jacket. He needed his hands warm . . .

What rotten luck again! There were lights topping the opposite hill.

With a bitter taste in his mouth, he turned, grabbed a handful of wet buckbrush, pulled himself up the steep bank, and disappeared.

From inside her car, Linda watched the approaching vehicle first with disbelief, then with a terrible anxiety. Who was it? Who was it?

Suddenly she realized that though her flashers were still flashing, her headlights were off. She scrabbled with numb fingers, found the switch, and pulled them on. In their abrupt brilliance she saw the approaching car was a truck, red and shiny with moisture. It was slowing, pulling over to her side of the road.

The cab door opened. A red-capped figure, with a denim jacket, turned up collar, half swung down, cautiously. A voice called, ''Hey, need some help?'' Then it said, ''Linda!''

Will Westerson slammed his truck door, jumped down, and ran clumsily through the sucking mud. By the time he'd reached the Chevy, Linda, in a stunning surge of relief, had unlatched her own door and had it half open. The dome light came on. He saw her dirty, tear-streaked face, her muddy wet clothes, and again said, ''Linda!'' deep in his throat. Suddenly icy with fear, he reached inside, yanking her toward him, gripping her shoulders, shaking her. His voice was harsh with demand. ''What's happened? Are you all right? Damn it, woman, talk to me!''

The tears were running again, making clean stripes on her dirty face. She opened her mouth, stammered through chattering teeth, ''I had a flat—I was fixing it—then there was a man—''

''Oh no!'' It was a groan. He caught her up, inside his big coat, holding her against his warm chest, wrapping the fleece lining around them both, rocking her. ''All right, all right, baby, it's all right now, it doesn't matter, you're safe, I've got you—''

He'd misunderstood. She knew he'd misunderstood, and for a moment it was so easy, so sweet to snuggle even closer, to take the warmth of his body, the litany in her ear.

But she couldn't. She mustn't.

She freed her head from his shoulder, looked up under dripping tresses, and said desperately, ''No—no—I ran—I looked up and he was there—on the bank—and I ran, I got in the car and drove—I got stuck, it wouldn't go, it simply wouldn't go— and you came—oh, Will, I am so glad you came, I was so scared—''

''Get in the cab.''

His voice had suddenly gone so calm. So stern.

She stammered, "W—what?"

"Get in the cab of my truck. Lock the doors."

He was already moving, half carrying her across the rutted verge, boosting her upward. "Hand me that flashlight. There. By your knee."

It was large, a foot long. Its beam cut the darkness to size, to reason. Brush became brush again, trees, trees, as he moved the light up along one bank, across the road, and down the other. Almost hypnotized, her eyes followed fearfully, fence post by fence post—

"There he is!"

She said the words out loud in a sort of horrifed bubble. The flashlight beam riveted, piercing the gossamer net of drifting fog, and the world stood still for five seconds.

Then it began again, slowly. Her voice shaking, she whispered, "Oh, Will—is that what I saw? I feel like such a fool—it looked so real, and I saw it—I thought I saw it move—"

His hand reached up and covered her cold one, but the other kept the light directly up the bank where the tall, crooked fence post stood silhouetted. It was braced on both sides, and wore a sodden cap of an empty, upside down herbicide sack.

"It probably was," he said gently, softly, trying to satisfy himself. "There's a bag like that about every fifty, sixty feet. It helps you keep count when you're spreading."

"But the noise—I heard him coming in the brush—"

"I have cattle in the cornfield, now. Could you have heard one of them? They sound like two-ton trucks."

He was being so calm, trying so hard to be nice when he so easily could have laughed. She drew a long, shuddering breath, remembering the cow that *had* scared her, until she'd seen it above her on the bank. She said, "Will, Will, what can I say? I really thought—I did—and I was terrified—"

He looked up at her; she caught the gleam of dark gray eyes beneath his cap, saw wet shining on his moustache and his mouth—not smiling. Not even the hint of a smile. He said, "Don't think you're the only one in the world to ever get scared. And I'm not saying you saw a fence post. I'm saying you *could* have. This is too funny a world, anymore, to take chances. Now sit tight. Lock the door. I'm going to see if I can get your car out without pulling it.''

She swallowed hard and obeyed.

The cab was blessedly warm, throwing heat on her wet, torn pants legs. The windshield had misted over. She turned the wiper switch. Through the clean fan shape on the glass she watched his stocky figure in its heavy jacket cross the road, then dip his head, and slide into her Chevy.

Had she seen a fence post and been scared by another cow? She knew about the herbicide bags. Every farmer upended them like that; all along the highways they could be spotted, mile after mile. And there had been one cow. She knew there'd been one cow. . . .

Steam spurted from the Chevy tailpipe in a jet, and the car began to rock, gently, persistently, back and forth, back and forth. Suddenly, with a grand spume of mud, gravel, and torn pigweed ejecting from its back wheels, it lurched up back onto the roadbed and stopped.

He let it run a moment, putting it into park and turning on the heater. Then he slid out, slamming the door with a solid ''thunk,'' ran back to his truck, head turtled into his collar against the wet, and opened the truck door. ''Move over,'' he said, and swung himself up beside her.

''Damn,'' he said. ''Nasty out there. Feeling better?''

''Some.''

''You really scared me!''

''I scared *you*!'' Then despite herself, she shivered. When he'd climbed in, she'd moved to the other side. The truck was old, the right door ill-fitted, and there was a cold draft. Helplessly, she shivered again and couldn't stop. ''Damn,'' she muttered between her teeth, trying to get over the chill, trying to not let him see.

That was useless. What he couldn't see he could feel. ''Hey, come here!'' he said and swept her inside his fleecy coat again, holding her tightly against his chest, wrapping the denim jacket about both of them. He began rocking her, as one rocks a child, murmuring soothing words—but she wasn't a child. She wasn't at all. And suddenly he was terribly, enormously aware that she wasn't.

He said shakily, "Linda?" And there was a tone to his deep voice, a sound she'd never heard before, a calling that made her blood stir. Her emotions were out of control, disconnected from her reasoning brain. She put her arms around him beneath his coat, clinging mindlessly.

He was so solid, so comforting. She needed him. She needed that sound in his voice. She answered it, moving her head, sending her soft mouth along the hard, stubbled line of his jaw until it found his mouth beneath the wet moustache—found his mouth searching for hers.

Outside, the rain beat against the cab windows, the heavy thrum of the truck engine hummed beneath their feet. But inside she felt only her wet body against his, the pounding of his heart, the complete rapture of his mouth.

No. No. No. Not complete. Not complete, yet. But it would be. It would be.

He turned his head, said against her throat, "Linda, I knew I wanted you, but I didn't know—I never imagined—that I wanted you like this, like now—"

He stopped, put a clamp on himself. Hard. Some things were too precious to rush. This was one of them. "We have to get you dry," he said unsteadily into the top of her wet head. "What I don't want is you with pneumonia. In a minute, sweetheart, I'll turn your car around and you can follow me home."

Suddenly she remembered, and the shock hit, jerking her back into hard reason with memory's awful claws. Home! She leaned back, pulling her wet arms away, feeling the cold on them from the drafty door, wiping awkwardly at her streaked and muddy face. Shakily, "Thanks for the invitation, but I don't think the woman you already have at home will care for the idea.''

His face went blank. ''What?'' And then he remembered too. He grimaced, ''Oh, Lord. Doris. I forgot about Doris.''

''Obviously!'' She was functioning again. Not terribly well, but she was functioning. ''Well, I'd forgotten about her too, for a minute. But I remember now. And if you think I'm going to get involved in some kind of wierdo threesome, Will Westerson, you're wrong . . . you are so wrong.''

His anger was rising with her own, but he forced himself to answer calmly, ''Linda, Linda, I never thought that for a minute. You know I didn't mean that. You don't understand about Doris, she's an old friend. A really sweet girl . . .''

The ''sweet girl'' bit, he saw immediately, was a terrible mistake. Linda's face clouded with fury again, and he too lost his temper, feeling cheated and furious at the whole screwed-up mess. ''Come on, Linda! I'm not going to sit here in a grain truck justifying my whole life before I met you! That would be stupid! I won't do it. But it *was* before I met you, and it's all over now. It's over with Doris.''

''Apparently you haven't told her that!'' It came out louder than she intended, but she was fighting tears. She slammed out of the truck and stalked to her own car. He moved to follow her, then changed his mind.

As she drove away, the tears began in earnest. She wiped at them clumsily with one dirty hand. Trying to decide which was worse, her disappointment or having made a fool of her self in front of that woman—sweet girl, ha!—in Will's house, Linda suddenly remembered Tony.

Tony was in *her* house.

It struck her like a blow. If her ex-husband's presence were to come to Will's attention, he might think . . . just as she had thought . . . that had never entered her mind, not until this second. She cried all the harder.

Making the turn onto the main road, she didn't notice the

old Ford, parked in the grass next to a bean field. The man in the car was cold, wet, frustrated, and beginning to lose the tight control he'd been keeping on his building anger. Linda didn't see the Ford ease out onto the pavement and begin to follow her again.

Chapter Ten

HALFWAY DOWN THE lane, Will slowed up and took another look at the situation. He had been more than ready to tell Doris off and put her on the road for St. Louis. But to be fair, this was not all Doris's fault. When she had showed up that afternoon, he didn't exactly throw her out on her ear. And speaking of ears, his own were beginning to burn, cold as they were. What had Linda and Doris said to each other about him?

As for why Linda had been there in the first place, part of that was answered as he started across his drive, put one foot on a spilled carton of potato salad, and saw another carton seeping baked beans from a tattered grocery bag.

She'd brought him dinner. She'd come out from town with stuff to feed him. And he hadn't been home. But Doris had.

As a kid on the farm in the bitter wintertime, he had often dressed in front of the big old parlor heater. That's how he felt right now—hot on one side and cold on the other.

Old Bowser was waiting patiently on the step. As Will approached, he stretched his creaky legs and wagged his tail. Will patted him and thought wryly, *Well, at least somebody loves me*, then amended the thought. *That's not precisely the problem, is it?*

He let Bowser in on the back porch, shucked off his muddy boots, and padded through the kitchen. Something smelled pretty good, but he wasn't hungry anymore—especially when he noted the table in the dining room set for two and candles burning in his mother's silver candlesticks.

Doris heard him. She rose from the couch with a whisper of drapery, and the costume she wore left little to the imagination. But he was seeing it all as it must have looked to Linda.

The expression on his face told Doris the evening was not going to go as she'd planned. It wasn't a big surprise. He'd not been exactly delighted to see her before. And then there'd been the gal with the grocery sack. Doris concluded it was time to cut her losses. She sighed, smiled with bright bravado, and said, "Now for my next magic trick—the reappearing bathrobe."

While she was shrugging on his tatty old dressing gown, Will decided he definitely did need a drink. He went to the old, curved oak china cupboard where he kept his Scotch, reached for it, then changed his mind. He turned to face Doris, sighing.

She was hugging the robe to her with folded arms. Suddenly he noticed the dark marks beneath her eyes. She looked tired. Soberly she said, "So I messed up."

He sat down, thrust his long wet legs out in front of him, and said, "No, no, I did. It's not your fault."

"Yes, it is. I didn't have to be playing the Samson and Delilah bit. We never needed that, Will. I guess I've spent too much time with Tony."

"Then why the hell were you playing it?"

"I wanted something."

"Come off it, Doris. Have you ever had to do more than just ask? You said it, yourself. We never played games!" He swallowed, lowered his voice. "What was it?"

"Nothing."

"That's a stupid answer. You're not stupid. And we're friends, Dorrie. We're still friends, I hope, although I'm mad as hell. What is it?"

She went to the window. The curtains were limp, and dead flies litered the sill. A housekeeper he wasn't. Looking out, she saw rain dripping from sodden trees under scudding clouds and a half moon. The dark shapes of cattle moved restlessly in a barn lot; beyond the cattle was a fence, then another fence, then more trees, tangling their bare branches against lingering patches of mist. Not a light in sight. Not a store, a marquee, a high-rise—not even a traffic signal. Pure desolation.

She shivered. She didn't like it here. She'd never liked it
here. No kid could change that. Kids could grow up in a city.
She had. It hadn't hurt her.

"I'm going to have a baby," she said.

Behind her there was a short thick silence while the anger
died. "Mine?" he asked quietly.

There's your chance, lady, she told herself. She didn't want
it. "No."

"Your airplane jockey's?"

"Yes."

"Have you told him?"

"No. He won't want it."

There was another small silence. He looked at her straight
back, the shape of fists knotted deep in his bathrobe pockets.
He felt compassion, but that was all. He said gently, "I want a
kid, Dorrie. Sometime. But not yours."

Her shoulders lifted, fell. "I was going to tell you."

"I hope so."

She swung around suddenly and faced him with fierce eyes.
"Damn it! Will, I want this baby!"

"Damn it, yourself. Have it, then. We'll all help. You know
that. You've got friends—good friends!"

"I also have this middle-class compulsion to give it a father."

"*That's* something you'll have to work on, yourself."

She almost smiled. "I was."

She turned back to the window, straightened the dusty curtains, pleating them with her fingers. "Will—"

"What?"

"Was that girl someone special?"

"Yes. At least—I thought so."

"I'm really sorry. I feel awful. What can I do?"

The obvious was that she'd done quite enough already. He
shrugged because the edge was still numb; it wasn't cutting
yet. "Hell. I don't know. Probably nothing."

"Could I talk to her? I would. I'd be glad to try."

"We'll work it out. If there's anything left to work."

That hurt, although he hadn't meant it to hurt her. She asked, "What's her name?"

But he was asking over her, "You want a drink?"

"No. Yes."

"Okay. Fix two, while I get out of these clothes."

"You want your bathrobe?"

Heaving himself to his feet, he almost grinned. "No, thanks. You can keep it. I'll manage."

He pulled on dry jeans and a T-shirt, came back in toweling his head, and took the Scotch-and-water she handed him.

She sipped hers and asked again, "What's her name?"

"Who?"

"Your girl's. The one I scared off."

"Oh. Linda. Linda Pietra."

She said, "Oh no." She said it very softly.

He had inhaled his drink. He shoved the empty glass at her, "That's pretty fair. I'll have another."

"You'll get bombed."

"You're right."

"Will you eat something if I fix another one?"

"I don't know. Maybe. Maybe not."

"Will, getting drunk won't help."

"Lady, with your screwed up life, you think you can unscrew mine? Make the drink."

She made it. Casually she asked, "Pietra. Is that any relation to Tony Pietra?"

"His ex. Although I've never met the lad myself. He's an airline—"

He stopped. He turned and looked at Doris closely. He said, "It isn't. It can't be."

She was turning her glass in her hands. She said, "When you said her name, I didn't believe it either. If this was a novel, I'd throw it halfway across the room. And right now if you say one single thing about a 'small world,' I'll split your head."

He was staring, aghast. "Your fly boy is Tony Pietra."

"At the risk of being redundant—he is, indeed."

He shrugged big shoulders, wiping a hand through tousled hair. "I gather you don't want to marry him."

She drained her own glass. "You've got it in one. The only way I'd take Tony Pietra would be on a platter with an apple in his mouth. At least Linda and I have that in common—besides you. And I gather that as far as you're concerned, she has dibs."

"If she still wants me."

"Don't be maudlin. She will. Eat a sandwich and go to bed."

She fixed it for him, ham with horseradish—the way he liked them. As he chewed morosely, she said, "Oh, I almost forgot. The sheriff's office called, said they ran a make on that license plate you gave them. It's registered to a Joey something. Brachetti. Joey Brachetti. So now they're trying to find a connection between Brachetti and the body they found over in someone's pasture. I thought you were through with copping, Westerson."

"It's the firehorse syndrome." He was saying *Brachetti, Brachetti* to himself, but it didn't equate with the tall man in the Ford. And suddenly an enormous yawn almost washed him away. Watching him struggle with his fatigue, Doris decided there was no use telling him about Slit. Not tonight. Maybe not at all. After all, he'd said he's out of it.

For some reason she thought of John Elman, then, probably still sitting at that cluttered desk where she'd left him earlier, the shirt buttoned around his lean middle with only half a button, and taking off those horn-rims to rub tired dark eyes . . . Then she remembered something else: "Oh. One thing more."

"What?"

"They said they still had somebody's glasses."

"Oh. Yeah. I forgot."

"Bully. I hope he can see without them."

He didn't answer. He was just sitting there like a lump. She gathered up the sandwich plate and the crumpled napkin and said wearily, "That's all. Go to bed."

He heaved himself erect, looked at her out of sunken eyes. "I'm sorry, Dorrie," he mumbled, not knowing for sure what he was sorry for.

She knew. She shrugged, said, "Sure. It's okay."

Night wind hit the old farmhouse, making the loose panes rattle. By the back fence, feeling a primal urge, a cow mooed hopefully to the lordly bull on the next farm. To Doris, the sound could have been a wild bear and she shuddered. She wondered how anyone could stand this place. She'd go nuts in a week.

She made another sandwich and ate it, sitting at the table between the two half-melted candles, watching them gutter and thinking her own thoughts.

She thought of John Elman, whose wife could never have kids, who melted every time some dirty-faced urchin turned up lost and teary at the precinct.

She remembered Will's words about having friends. She'd really done an awful thing to Will. Could she straighten it out? She hated meddlers. But was this meddling? Probably, she nodded to herself, and decided to do it anyway. Anything would be better than sitting in this dark dump all night listening to weird noises. At least the little town had streetlights.

She changed back into her slacks and sweater, repacked her bag, and looked up Linda Pietra's address in the phone book.

Bowser padded quietly in from the back porch as she opened the door, and he headed for his favorite night spot beside Will's bed. Dorrie patted him on the head as he passed and told him, "Take good care of Will, Rover. He's a good man."

Outside, she scrambled into her mist-covered Trans Am and jammed down the door locks. Whatever that bulk was against the fence, it wasn't going to get the big brave police lady now!

When the Trans Am left, Will heard it. He wasn't asleep. Sleep, as it often did, had fled when his head touched the pillow. But he saw no value in trying to stop Doris; when a thing was over it was over.

Wow, Westerson, you're really profound, he thought dryly.

He hoped that Doris, after all, knew she could count on him in the clutch.

Feeling the beginnings of a stomachache, Will got up, fell over Bowser, apologized, took an Alka Seltzer, went back to bed, and stared up at the ceiling again.

Tomorrow he'd find Linda. He'd make her listen. Right now, he reasoned, thrashing over and pillowing his aching head on a bare arm, he couldn't do a damned thing. So he may as well think of something else.

Like Joey Brachetti. Who was he? The body in the pasture? If so, and if the tall guy was driving his car, then the guy had dropped Brachetti. Okay.

So why was he still hanging around?

Because he wasn't finished, yet.

Now there was a big fat chill.

If he wasn't finished yet, then someone else was due to buy it. Someone here. In this area.

Who around here could be important enough to rate a hit man from St. Louis?

Then it came on him like a restful blanket: *It's not your problem, Westerson!*

And he finally went to sleep.

Chapter Eleven

THERE IS ONE fact recognized by most wearers of contact lenses, to wit—it's not too bright to leave them in when you cry.

By the time Linda had reached the outskirts of Penfield her burning eyes were giving her fits. She had to get her contacts out. Also, she needed a phone. Damn Tony. She couldn't walk into her apartment looking like a drowned rat. Rather, she *wouldn't*. Tony might decide to be comforting, and she just wasn't up to a hassle.

She pulled into the Conoco station and was half out of the car before she saw the out-of-order sign on the telephone. Damn, again. But there was another down the street on the edge of the courtyard—if she didn't have to fight the kids for it.

She didn't. The night, so far, had been too cold and wet to lounge on the park benches.

She parked her car in front of the bank, wiped at tears that were streaming now from irritation, grabbed her bag, and hurried across the street.

The booth light was out and the phone book gone, but a distant streetlamp barely lit the dial and she knew Karen's number. Karen understood about Tony; she'd put her up for the night.

Karen's number was busy.

Meaning to try again shortly, Linda occupied her time in searching her bag for her contact lens case. Vaguely she knew that another car had pulled in behind hers. It was an old one and had one man in it—a big one.

About the size of my fence post feedbag, she thought, totally without humor. His door was opening, so she supposed he wanted to use the telephone, too. Well, he'd just have to wait!

She got one lens out, dropped it in its little cell and snapped the lid. Now the world was not only bleary, it was fifty per cent fuzz. Removing the second lens made it one hundred percent. Thank God she had her glasses in the car.

Across the street, the blurred man swung his feet out, stood up. But before he could step away from his door a second car screeched in behind him, and from it a fat lady teetered across the street in a flutter of scarves, beads, and blowsy kiss-curls. With a look of annoyance on her blush-painted cheeks, she tapped imperatively on the glass door.

Linda was in no mood to be pushed around. She smiled sweetly, jammed her foot against the hinge so it wouldn't open, and calmly redialed Karen.

Not busy now. Just no answer.

The fat lady tapped the glass impatiently with a brightly polished fingernail. Perversely, Linda blinked back the overflow in her abused eyes, squinted, and dialed the Bellam's. She hoped Ron was home. He was.

"Hi. This is Linda. May I ask a favor?" She told him only that she'd had a flat, had to change it, then explained about Tony.

He laughed. "Sure, come on over. In fact, I'm glad you're coming. I have to go to work, and Sue's parents are on the way. If you're here, you can tell them where I am and I can go on."

So one problem was resolved.

Linda stepped out of the phone booth, gave the impatient lady a sweet smile, and squished across the street to her car. The big man had apparently decided it was going to be a long wait. He was sitting patiently in the shadows. Linda gave him the vague smile people in small towns bestow on strangers, got into the Chevy, and rummaged for her glasses.

With them on her nose again, the world resumed its normal clarity. She put the car in gear and drove away without another thought for the man behind her.

She was, however, prominent in the thoughts of the man.

Lights were on all over the Bellam apartment, and Ron met her at the door. He was in a fresh uniform, his dark hair damp from the shower and his grin enormous.

"Hi," he said. "Boy, are you a mess! I'm glad Pussycat's still over at Mrs. Thomas's; he'd probably try to hide you under the porch."

Linda answered, "Thanks, officer, I really needed that. Isn't your shift over?"

"Extra duty. They're setting roadblocks, looking for some guy."

Lightly she asked, "Anybody I know?" Still, for some reason she glanced back over her shoulder at the empty verandah, yellow beneath the porchlight, and the black, glistening tatters of spirea that edged it. There was a cold, raw pungency of wet wood in the air, and silence. Absolute silence. As though even the birds were huddled, listening. The only thing moving was one car, far down the street, and as she watched, even it stopped, turning its headlights off, becoming just a darker shadow in a mass of shadows.

Why in the world did she have the sense of eyes watching her? And how ridiculous could she get? This was Penfield—safe and sane Penfield—caught, in many ways, in the archaic web of the fifties. She gave herself a shake. She needed to get cleaned up and start dealing with her problems. Beginning with Tony, damn him. Right now she needed Tony Pietra like she needed a disease.

Ron was answering her question, saying, "This guy is no one you know—unless you've been consorting with hoods and other lowlife." He followed her across the dim light of the oaken foyer and into his own bright, warm living room.

"Got to remember that hall chandelier needs another bulb," he said. "I think they're all burnt out but one, and we don't need Colonel Thomas breaking his neck trying to replace them."

She nodded, pulled off her wet shoes, and sighed at the muddy, bedraggled bottoms of her slacks. "Do you have some kind of eyewash? I left my contacts in too long or got something in them when I changed the tire. It was foul out there.''

He'd picked up his trooper hat, put it on, and said, ''Let's have a look.'' He guided her to the bright floor lamp by the window with its drawn blind and, bending close, inspected each eye. ''You've met Sue's folks?''

''Yes. Last Fourth of July. Do you see anything?''

''Just eyeball. Watermelon pink. Wait—'' He took both hands and tilted her head. ''No, I guess not. I thought I saw a speck, but I didn't. Anyway, tell them to take the bedroom. I'll take the hide-a-bed in the nursery. And you're welcome to the couch if you want to stay.''

''I might. Thank you.''

''It's the least I can do for a prospective godparent. Oh, the Thomas's are going to keep Pussycat for a while. He wants to come home, but my father-in-law is a dog man, and Sue's mother can find cat hairs the minute she steps across the threshold. I swear she attracts them like lint.'' He turned away, picked up a jacket, opened the door. ''I wish I knew when I'd be home, but I really can't say. This guy they're looking for—St. Louis seems to want him pretty bad. It appears that wherever he turns up somebody gets quietly decimated.''

''How come he's loose?''

''They've never been able to hang anything on him.''

''He sounds competent.''

''You could call it that.''

Ron's voice was wry, but Linda's thoughts were far away from the reality of death and killing. She shivered and sneezed, and he forgave her for her temporary fit of self-absorption; it was hard to debate humanity's frailties when you were wet to the fanny with mud. He said kindly, ''Get in the shower. I'll see you later. Make yourself at home.''

She sneezed again. ''Tell Sue hello. Kiss them both for me.''

''Gladly,'' he grinned.

The door closed behind him.

Silence fell again. A thick, full silence. Strange. Silence had never bothered her before. Nor being alone. In fact, after finally getting away from Tony Pietra's three-ring-circus life, she'd loved being alone, loved not having to answer to anyone but herself, loved not being pulled hither and yon by things beyond her control.

That was one of the things she'd shared with Will. Both of them had been raised to be independent; Linda, because her mother was an invalid and her father often gone on a flight, and Will because of growing up on a farm. And they'd both finally made big changes in the way they lived—both had given up and run, in fact. Although her running had been blind and Will's calculated.

As for being alone right now, it had a new meaning. *You've been an idiot,* she told herself crossly. *And when you've been an idiot, you have to face it. Being by yourself makes you think about it. Worse, you have to concede that you're a losing idiot, and you've never been able to handle losing.*

She needed to do something positive, like getting cleaned up before Sue's parents arrived. But as a small concession to her uneasy feeling, she crossed the shag rug and pulled down both pairs of window blinds.

Mindful of the impending arrival of the new grandparents, she hurried out of her wet, muddy clothes and into the warm shower. Still she couldn't shake her vague apprehension.

She tried to think about something else. Sue's baby. Books. Movies. The last topic called to mind the film called *Psycho*, in which the girl was knifed in the shower and blood ran down the drain . . .

She'd never realized before how vulnerable a person is in the shower. You can't hear and can hardly see. The naked body is so soft and defenseless . . .

What *was* the matter with her?

Feeling like a nincompoop but unable to stop the goose bumps, Linda groped for a towel, threw it around herself, and ran on bare, wet feet for the bedroom.

Trying hard to laugh at herself, she thought, *If that mouse of*

The "mouse," of course, was long gone from the closet. But neither was he that far away. And his temper had worsened. Once calm, cool, and efficient, he was now savage. Punitive.

He'd tried to put out of his mind the sound of the telephone burring away mechanically in an empty house. His empty house. By his empty bed, where his wife's silky, diaphonous nightgown lay across the rumpled satin sheets . . . or worse, much worse, on the floor by a bed that was not empty.

She wouldn't dare! She wouldn't dare do that, wouldn't dare take another man into his bed. He'd kill her, she knew he'd kill her! Yet the idea almost drove him berserk. He was no longer a cold machine; he was a bomb, ready to explode.

He sat in his car parked down the street in the shadows, feeding his own jealousy on the sight of the silhouettes against the apartment lamplight, embracing. He tried hard to focus on what he should be thinking about—getting to the girl. Only the girl was his concern.

One of the most dangerous things in his line of work was emotion. He knew it. He tried to stifle his. He didn't quite succeed. He looked at his strong, curved fingers and knew what he wanted—a woman's throat between them. A look of terror on a woman's face. Any woman. Any. They were all the same. They were all sneaky, conniving . . .

The cop was leaving!

Narrow-eyed, Slit watched the man run down the steps and slide into his car. The yard light caught his face, showed it smiling, smug. He waited until the cop car had gone out of sight around the corner and the street was silent. His wristwatch said a little after ten.

Unmoving, eyes narrowed, he studied the house with disapproval. A sagging old turreted monster—must cost a fortune to heat—surrounded by unshaped shrubbery and antiquated, dim pole lights. With pride, he thought of his own tidy split-level, set in the middle of its clipped emerald lawn, with the patio out back and two built-in gas grills. No toys or tricycles messing up his grass.

This place was an eyesore. And besides, it gave him the creeps. All small towns gave him the creeps.

He opened the car door, listening. No sounds except a stupid night bird squawking crossly in a fir tree by the drive. Typical small town bird without sense enough to go to sleep, he thought. Undisciplined like everything else. Slit liked things that moved in regular patterns; then a guy knew where he was. Quiet as a mountain lion, he crossed the wet lawn into the shadows of the house. For a moment he glimpsed his quarry, but wasn't disturbed when she drew the blinds. Fine. He didn't need an audience.

But he had one. Three kids were coming down the street. They all had UNICEF cans, and one was holding the little twerp in the Charlie Daniels hat by the arm, half dragging him along. A brown mutt trotted at their heels.

Cursing silently, Slit pressed himself into the corner behind the wet spirea bushes where a bay window jutted. His feet disturbed a mole's run, loosing a fine smell of moldy earth. As the boys went by, the mutt's ragged ears perked. He lingered to make a small series of forays into the spirea, not quite daring to snap at the man's muddy pants legs. Slit stared balefully at the scruffy dog, thinking how much he'd like to dispose of it, and how he might do it.

Fortunately, one of the boys looked back and called disgustedly, "Come on, Prince! Whatever it is, let it alone!"

The Charlie Daniels hat started back, tugging at the hand that held him. "What's he got? Leggo! I wanna see!"

His captor growled, "You're going to see, all right! You're going to see plenty and feel more when Mom hears what you've been up to! Knock it off!"

The dog hesitated. Perhaps he was an obedient dog. Or perhaps he sensed that he was not totally welcome in his current surroundings. Whatever the reason, with one last "Burf!," he turned with his tail insouciantly erect and rejoined the juvenile platoon.

The Hat and his brother went up the steps of the house next door, closing it firmly behind them. The others, dog following, loafed on down the street and turned the corner.

Slit drew a deep, cautious breath and cursed hick towns and parents who allowed their children to roam the streets at ten o'clock at night. He stepped away from the spireas, glanced up and down the sidewalk.

Empty.

He'd better move while it was.

With the comfortable gait of a man heading home, he went up on the porch, opened the door, and stepped into the dim foyer.

Just in time.

He didn't notice, but the mutt named Prince had returned. He came bounding up on the porch just as the door closed.

Experience had taught the dog that what went in eventually came out. He'd wait. He had nothing else particularly pressing. Calmly curling into a compact ball, he put his nose on his tail and composed himself for what might be a lengthy vigil.

He was a new dog in the neighborhood. He hadn't learned yet about Pussycat.

Before long a car pulled into the drive, disgorging people and luggage. The dog rose to greet them, wagging his tail cheerfully.

"Hullo there, boy, are you the welcoming committee?" the man said.

"Don't jump on me, puppy." The woman was less pleased to see the dog. "Open the door, George, before I drop something. You'll have to make two trips; I couldn't carry the picnic basket."

Inside the foyer, Slit's hand, gently easing open the apartment door, froze in disbelief. This was incredible! One simple operation and every time he moved he was screwed!

His legs were long. They took the oak staircase upward into shadows in three strides. From the landing, in the sheltering dark, he looked down on the two people entering the house, both of them loaded down with luggage and grocery sacks. The dog was dancing around their feet, and the woman was squealing, "Go away! Go away! Oh, hello, Mrs. Thomas. Is this your dear doggie? Have you heard about Sue? Isn't it marvelous? Linda, darling, would you help daddy with the suitcases, how nice to see you again. . . ."

Mrs. Thomas closed her door firmly on Pussycat's indignant whiskers and embraced Sue's mother, luggage, and all. The air was full of "only four hours labor—why, with my Brian I was—" and "—a precious little girl, I hope Ronnie wasn't disappointed; he didn't sound disappointed, did he, daddy?"

The man winked at Linda, handed her his load, said, "No, dear, he didn't sound disappointed," and went back out for more. Linda, her hair still damp and her dry body encased a little snugly in a pair of Sue's prepregnancy jeans, ushered both chattering ladies into the Bellam apartment, excluding the dog with a skillful foot.

In the momentary hiatus, above them, Slit stared in disbelief. They were moving in! The old duffer and his wife had come to stay—at least the night and, from the amount of luggage, probably until the next century!

Here came the man again, with a wicker basket, a thermos, and a plastic bag of bread. He opened the apartment door calling, "Gangway. As you can see, girls, mother is not going to let Ron starve while Sue's away. Move, dog."

Once again the door shut.

Disappointed, but with resurgent cheerfulness, the brown mutt sat down, scratched his ear with one hind leg, arose, put both front paws on the bottom step of the stairway and looked up. His nose wiggled inquiringly.

Once more, that strangely indefinable aura of unfriendliness drifted down.

Okay. So he wouldn't go up there. But neither could he back out until someone opened the door again.

For the first time he noticed a rather positive smell of cat. Well. All right. If there was a pecking order in this neighborhood, he may as well get it established now as later. He plopped down to wait on the worn tile floor with a solid ''flump.'' But he didn't close his eyes. The smell was pretty strong, and you can't trust a cat.

Upstairs in the dark, Slit discovered with dismay that both upper apartment doors were solidly locked, as was the window at the end of the hall. Trapped. What went up had to, perforce, go down.

Quietly, he started his descent. The dog watched with interest, not moving. However, as Slit's gum-rubber soled foot passed within a foot of his nose, he stood up—cautiously. Instinct told him that this man was not friendly, but he *was* going toward the door. Surely he wouldn't mind sharing an exit.

Meanwhile, inside Mrs. Thomas's apartment, Pussycat had sat staring resentfully at the barrier between himself and home. He reached out a tentative paw and made a discovery. The door was shut but not latched. Industriously he went to work with paws and teeth. It was the labor of just a few minutes, but as the door edged obligingly open, the raffish tom saw not freedom but the passing legs of his old enemy from the closet!

With the frightful snarl of a miniature puma, he launched himself.

From the corner of his eye, Slit glimpsed the black-and-white furred projectile. Instinctively he threw up one arm to protect himself, reaching with the other for the front door. The door stuck on the first tug, and Pussycat got in some good licks on the same previously lacerated limb before the door finally opened. The cat bounced off the stair banister where he was flung full force, rolled on the tile, and came smack up against the paws of a frozen and thoroughly confused dog.

The second line of action started immediately and resulted in sufficient battle sounds to cover those of Slit's feet, pounding off the porch and into the bushes.

In a matter of minutes Linda, Sue's parents, and Mrs. Thomas separated cat from dog; the dog galloped up the street minus a few fur patches and very depressed in his mind, and Pussycat was confined, fizzing and yowling, to the kitchen. Slit sat in the Ford, winded, bleeding and—worst of all—routed.

Routed. Impossible. It couldn't happen to him. A hick town and a hick broad. It mustn't happen.

The blood was hammering in his ears, and there were new, deep scratches down his forearm, oozing damply through his jacket sleeve. He dabbed with the same handkerchief as before, already brown with dried blood from the first time.

Not for ten years had the awful thought entered his mind that was entering it now—the possibility of failure! The possibility of not finishing a job!

He had to stay cool. Think. Use his head.

He had to get that broad alone. By herself. Away from every-body. But how?

He thought a moment, tongue flicking dry lips.

Then he had it. He knew. He knew how.

He started his car, backed around, and headed for the motel on the edge of this twelfth-century anthill. He was going to have to wait a little, and he might as well be comfortable while he waited.

Chapter Twelve

AFTER THE MAN at the gas station directed her to Piper Lane, Linda's apartment house wasn't too hard to find. Doris parked next to a small Datsun, took a deep breath, and went up the open stairs to the row of orange doors on the second floor. Linda's was the third orange door. Doris hesitated, gritted her teeth, and knocked on it.

When Tony Pietra answered, she nearly fell off the balcony—which was nothing compared to Tony's reaction.

He paled, hissed, "Don't you know they could follow you?" and yanked her inside.

She almost knocked over a lamp as she tried to get her balance. Grabbing it as it teetered, she cried indignantly, "Tony, what's wrong with you? What are you doing?"

"What's it look like? I'm chain-locking the door. You may have led them straight to me!"

"Led who? You're not making sense. First I'd have to know you were here—which I didn't. I came to see Linda."

He'd dashed into the kitchen, locked that door, and came back. The name *Linda* stopped him dead. Unbelieving, he echoed, "Linda!"

His face changed. "Why do you want to see Linda?" Black brows drew down. In a soothing, almost placating tone, he went on, "Look, Dorrie, sweetie, you don't understand. There's nothing going on between Linda and me. It's over. I promise . . ."

Exasperated, she wondered if her baby would much resemble its father. In a cross voice, she answered, "All right. I don't care. Listen to me carefully. Watch my lips. I . . . don't . . .

care. Although, I admit I am a little less eager to see Miss Purity now than I was a few minutes ago—finding you here.''

''That's why she isn't.''

''Isn't what? Wait. Don't answer that. Let me sit down, give me a cigarette, fix me a drink. Then we'll talk.''

She took the chair by the lamp, glanced around. A nondescript furnished apartment, but with two good pieces of furniture—one of them a walnut Victorian table—and some nice pictures on the opposite wall.

Tony offered her a Kool. She hated Kools. But she took it, lit, and inhaled blue smoke in a warm, comforting draft, while he went back into the kitchen where she heard the crack of ice-cube trays being emptied. He returned with a Scotch on the rocks, handed it to her, then stood like a little boy hauled on the carpet, his hands behind him, his face properly anxious.

She regarded him dispassionately, deciding that what she had just told him was, indeed, the truth. She really did not care. She took a sip of her drink. It was very good Scotch. Then she raised her eyes to his face.

He had his color back, but she could see his clasped hands in the mirror across the room, and his fingers were twiddling each other. Tony was nervous. In fact, Tony might even be scared. And, on a practical plane, certainly not about his tomcatting. He could lie his way out of that—he had for years. So, what else?

She said casually, ''Why are you here?''

''What?''

''Why are you here? You did say that Linda wasn't.''

''Yes. And I did say that's why she wasn't. Because I am. She's really not too fond of me anymore.''

''It may get to be a large club, Tony.''

That stung his ego. He frowned, ''Lay off, Dorrie. I have enough problems. If you didn't know I was here, then why are you in this godforsaken town?''

''Visiting a friend. Or, I was.''

''A friend!'' Then his face cleared. ''Oh. Westerson. He is

up here, isn't he? Okay. In fact—wow!'' He took a deep breath, puffing out both cheeks, and his hands relaxed. ''What a relief! I figured I was had. Damn, you scared me, kitten!''

She snuffed out the cigarette. ''All right,'' she said. ''Tell mama. What sort of trouble are you in this time? Why are you locking doors and who would I have led to you?''

He shuffled his feet and grimaced. ''It's really ridiculous. There's a guy missing. When they find him, he'll tell them I'm clean. But until they do, I'd rather they couldn't find me.''

''What guy?''

''You don't know him. His name is Joey Brachetti.''

Brachetti. Brachetti. She closed her eyes, said the name. She remembered. She said flatly, ''Surprise. I know the name. And I know they've found him.''

''Found him!''

''Somebody did. He's dead.''

Tony blanched, muttered an oath, and lit a cigarette with noticeably shaking hands. ''You're sure.''

''Reasonably. I heard it secondhand. Earlier today. Is that good news or bad?''

He flicked his lighter and stared at it with brows still knitted beneath the soft swing of black hair across his forehead. He answered slowly, ''I don't know. It depends on who found him. And if they found his books.''

''Books. Books? Oh. Great. You've been at the ponies again. You jerk. You didn't default on your bookie!''

''No, no, no.'' He said it indignantly, as though she'd impugned his honor. ''He did. I gathered that he hadn't paid the management's cut. When they went to lean on him, he wasn't there. So they were going around suggesting his customers pay again—until they found him, of course.''

''So you ran! Rather a guilty move, wasn't it, since you say you had paid?''

''I had. I paid, damn it! But I don't have that kind of money —not to pay twice. I have other obligations.''

She puffed her cheeks at that one. Probably he had, she

thought bitterly. But with the rest of his harem, not with her.

"And you think they'll come looking for you. Right?"

"I don't know. Not now, I don't. Now that you say he's dead. Anyway, they wouldn't find me here unless they followed you."

Now she was indignant. "Me! Why should they follow me?"

Uncomfortably, he answered, "You're one of my girl-friends."

In a dry voice she replied, "I'm everybody's girlfriend. Anyway, I expect you're off the hook since he's dead. The local dispatcher said it was beginning to look like a contract job, and if that's the case, then your poor bookie has been disciplined and the money's back. Relax."

She tried to take her own advice, leaning back and sipping at the scotch. Suddenly she was very, very tired. Rest. That's what she needed. In fact, she'd probably need a lot of it. She ought to cut down on the booze, too. And the smoking. This kid of hers was going to grow properly, not get his brains scrambled before he was even born.

She put down the glass, neatly, on a lucite coaster. "Okay, me bucko. Back to Page One. Where's Linda?"

"I have no idea. Out."

"Is she coming home tonight?"

"I don't know that. She has friends in this puddle of a town, I suppose. I crashed in on her unexpectedly. She probably had plans of her own. She didn't tell me."

Doris knew about the plans. What they had been. She closed her eyes, tried to think. Tony's voice, suddenly sharp, jabbed at her:

"Why do you want to know? You, of all people? Hey. What's going on here?"

"None of your business." She said it sharply. "Damn. I suppose I can see her in the morning."

"I suppose. She'll show up at work, if nothing else. Conscientious, that's my Linda. Dull. Uninspired. But conscientious. Are you still visiting your friend?"

"No."

"Going back to the city?"

"No. I told you, I want to see Linda. I'll find a motel."

"Good idea. I'll go with you."

"I didn't invite you."

He turned the charm up a watt. "Look, Dorrie, I've played ten thousand games of solitaire, watched nine hours of soap on the television, and read every label on the cans in the kitchen. I'm turning into a basket case. Have a heart."

He didn't reach out and touch her. That would have been a mistake.

You had to know how Dorrie worked. He did.

Instead, he went into the kitchen, wrote a note to Linda saying "See you in the morning," stuck it on the fridge, piled his dirty dishes in the sink for her, picked up his coat from the chair, and went back into the living room, saying cheerfully, "Got your Trans Am? I'll leave Penny's Datsun here and pick it up tomorrow."

She hadn't moved. She looked up at him thoughtfully. He was a good looking guy. Motel rooms could be awfully empty.

Why not?

"I'll drive," she said, and preceded him down the wooden steps in the damp, cool night air.

If they did follow him, he thought calmly as they drove off, they'd find the Datsun and think he was at Linda's. And tomorrow, if things looked a little antsy, he could go back to St. Louis in the Trans Am and bid that flight to Cairo . . .

If it occurred to him that he might be putting Linda in danger, he dismissed the idea. Years ago he decided to only worry about one thing at a time. And a guy had to look after Number One. No one else would.

Chapter Thirteen

FOURTEEN HOURS HAD now passed since Joe Brachetti had fallen with a gentle sigh, face down on the clover in a pasture twenty miles away. Fourteen hours—and Slit had not yet been able to get to the woman who could finger him.

It baffled him, it hurt his pride, and it bruised an ego already wounded. A hick town and a dumb broad had him by the short hairs—not with cunning, not with armed defense, but with simple bucolic bumbling. That, perhaps, was the worst.

They had a corpse, and they had a witness. They no longer had her film. It could easily be days before Joey was identified, and—being the hicks they were—their protection of their witness had been laughable.

So why wasn't he laughing?

Anyway, he'd spent enough time already in this little pig wallow of a place, where people didn't lock their doors and kids wandered home at ten o'clock and the guy at the motel desk didn't even blink when he paid cash for his room. Good God! If you offered cash in St. Louis, it not only scared them to death, but they didn't even quite know what to do with it! Proper people had one hand permanently curved to fit the size of a credit card. That's what Mona's friend said—the one who ran the fast-food place.

The thought of his wife brought the tightness back to his chest.

He washed up, cleaning out the deep, stinging scratches on his arm and chest, and putting on more of the first aid cream he'd taken from the broad's apartment earlier in the day.

Then he went back, sat on the side of the bed, and dialed. ''Credit card,'' he said, and used Joey's number again.

His home phone began its haunting ring, and he stared ahead with narrow, brooding eyes, at the drawn drapery.

''Hello.''

So she was home. But the voice was breathless. Why?

''Hello? Hello?''

''Hello, Mona.''

''Sweetheart, I've been so worried! I got the roses—they're beautiful—but I'd rather have you. Are you in town? Are you coming home? I have the champagne iced, and the kids are at mama's until tomorrow.'' Her voice dropped, turned sensuous. ''And I'm just here, darling, cuddled up in the fur bed-spread—waiting . . .''

Even her voice turned his guts to water, and the mental images she was conjuring up—they could destroy him.

She repeated, ''When are you coming home?''

Nothing she said now was beyond suspicion. Nothing. Why did she want to know when? So she could get that muscled stud out of there in time?

His voice expressionless, he asked, ''Where were you earlier?''

Now she'd caught a thread of something wrong. She said, ''Downtown. I said I'd get the champagne.''

''What car did you drive?''

''What car did I drive? Why—the Buick. Why?''

There had been a hesitation before she'd said *Buick*. He knew there'd been a hesitation. He answered, ''Just curious.'' Now let her worry about that.

She was. She asked, swiftly, ''What's wrong?''

''Nothing.''

''Are you in trouble?''

''No. But I think maybe you are,'' he said and he hung up.

Then he laid back across the bed and transferred his savage stare to the ceiling. He could imagine her now, frantically jiggling the telephone, calling his name. He knew that at this moment not even the fur bedspread could warm her, that she was cold with fear, that her eyes were darting wildly around the room like a cornered rabbit's. He'd been angry with her before. She knew what he did when he was angry with her. It wasn't nice.

But she wouldn't dare run away. He knew that, too. Because there was no place she could go he couldn't find. She'd just have to sit. And wait.

She didn't know how far away he was or when he'd come. He'd told her nothing except that he *knew*. Very good. Let fear eat at her mind as jealousy ate at his. Fair was fair.

Now he could put his thoughts on the business at hand: the broad in the yellow airplane.

He only needed to get close to her. A crowd would do. He'd dropped a guy on an escalator once and had been fifty feet away before he'd fallen. There's not much initial feeling with a knife, no whammo like a bullet plowing through you.

But he'd spent the entire day trying to get close. This hick town was like an ant farm—no big, surging masses, just people trickling here and yon, no pattern, just chance.

Chance, he couldn't afford. He was running out of time.

So. Back to the initial contact: the yellow airplane. The yellow airplane that was for sale—he'd seen the sign on its nose.

I have, he said to himself, *just become an airplane buyer,* and reached for the skinny phone book on the nightstand.

What he had in mind was high risk. But he lived with high risk; the key to success was thinking it through first, foreseeing all the contingencies. Primary was the danger of her recognizing him immediately. But he thought he had the answer to that—at least enough of an answer to buy just the amount of time needed to finish his chore. As an airplane buyer he'd be totally out of context—far, far from the category of murder or police or anything connected with that field across the river, Joey dead, and him looking up at her like a starstruck idiot.

Also, there were subtle ways of changing appearance and he knew them all. When he'd taken off after Joey, his glasses had been in his pocket and his jacket laid over the seat. So that part really didn't bug him too much. All he needed were the few seconds necessary to get close to her. Then, zap.

If this were St. Louis, he acknowledged to himself that it wouldn't be as easy. Lieutenant Elman was no country dumbo; he could readily envision Elman using the broad as bait and inviting a confrontation, so he could close in and trap the guy she could identify. But not here. Not in Podunk Center. They weren't even watching her.

Dandy. He was all for it. It made things a lot simpler for him. He'd been following her. That had been wrong. Now let her find him.

With the perfect confidence of having never failed, he ran his finger down the *B*s in the phone book. Bellam. There it was.

He dialed. It only rang once when a breathless voice said, "Bellam's."

"Mrs. Bellam?"

There was a small hesitation, almost as if his voice had been a disappointment. Then she answered, "This is Linda."

She started to say more, but he cut her off: "Fine. You're the one I want. You own the yellow airplane that's for sale?"

In the Bellam apartment, Linda's heart sank further into her soggy shoes. Tom said he'd had an inquiry. This must be it. Well, she had put it up for sale, and at that particular moment she was not inclined to keep anything that in anyway even vaguely smacked of Will Westerson!

She swallowed and answered, "Yes. The Cub."

But she didn't say anymore, and at his end of the line Slit thought in disgust that she'd make a hell of a poor salesman.

He asked, "Could I have a look at it?"

"Are you a pilot, Mr.—"

Two traps—name and occupation—and he'd fall into neither of them. "Black. Edwin Black; I travel with a St. Louis corporation. And no, I'm not a pilot. My son is." He had a quick, fond image of his four-year-old in Star Wars pajamas, zooming a plastic spacecraft around his bedroom. "If the airplane appears to be what he's looking for I'll tell him about it when I get home."

Linda's heart lightened. So nothing was imminent. No sale tomorrow that would be regretted the next day. Someone "just looking" and there were always plenty of those. In relief at postponing painful decision she answered almost cheerfully, "I'd be happy to show the Cub to you. Tomorrow morning? I usually fly about seven. If the weather's right."

Talk about candy from a baby!

"Earlier, if you don't mind," he said. "I should be in St. Louis by eight-thirty."

"That's fine. Six, then. I'll meet you by the Cub."

"Very good. Thanks. See you then."

He hung up, trying not to laugh. Talk about Simple Simon! No asking for credentials, no questions. She'd probably even take a check!

He got up, stretched, pulled off his pants and rubbed at the dried mud. Most of it came off on the carpet. Good. The balance of the wet had gone on Joey's poncho. He took a hot shower, cringing as the water washed the lacerations on his chest, put his shorts back on, found "Benny Hill" on Channel Eleven, slid into bed, doubled a pillow behind his head, and tried to watch it.

But the wrong images kept coming between his eyes and the screen. Mona. Mona.

A car door slamming caught his ear.

He was up in one smooth motion, gliding to the drapes, and the fabric didn't even move as he made a slit to see through.

A red Trans Am had parked next to his Ford, and a couple was going in next door. He'd never seen the man before, but the woman looked familiar. Unless he was getting hyper.

No. He wasn't. He had seen her.

But where?

He frowned, flipping files in his mind. Thirtyish, Farrah Fawcett hair, big boobs . . . .

They'd gone inside, out of sight.

Uneasy, he made certain of the lock on his door, went back to bed, but didn't stretch out again.

First the turkey in the blue shirt at the yard sale, then this bird next door.

Vaguely he could hear voices. He leaned over, put his ear against the wall. He caught the tone of their conversation and relaxed a little. Just a couple of people ready to have it off in a motel room then move on. No sweat.

The door to the next unit clicked open again, and heels tat-tatted on the concrete.

Slit hoisted himself erect and went back to the window.

The woman was getting a small suitcase out of the car. The guy must be standing in the doorway, because he heard him distinctly as he said, ''Why don't you call?''

''Call who?''

''Westerson. All you have to do is ask.''

''For crying out loud, Tony, Will's in bed. He's tired. He's working hard, trying to make his damned farm go.''

''It's only ten thirty, for Pete's sake!''

''In Pike County that's the middle of the night!''

''All I want to know is whether they found Joey's accounts with Joey! All I want to know is whether I can go to sleep tonight and be fairly sure of waking up tomorrow. Now is that unreasonable?''

She was coming back, carrying the case and a little dressing bag. She looked exasperated. ''Yes. Besides, Will's out of it. All he did was give them a license number. They ran a make on the plate and found out it was registered to Brachetti. End of story as far as Will is concerned. I don't think he even cares.''

The voices muffled again as the door closed.

But Slit was still standing thunderstruck by the window.

When had he had such rotten luck?

Westerson. Will Westerson. The turkey in the blue shirt.

An ex-cop.

Now he remembered him—too damned well.

And Westerson had remembered him—at least enough to be curious, enough to take down his license number.

Good sense told him he'd better bail out of this place. Pronto.

But he couldn't. The girl in the airplane could still finger him, ten years could still go down the tube, and worse, he could find himself doing time for murdering a small potato bookie no one really gave a damn about in the first place!

There was no other way. He had to wait until morning.

It might be the longest night of his life. He had to stay in control; he couldn't get the jumps. The car—the Ford—was parked out there in plain sight beneath the security light between the Trans Am and an LTD. He knew the best place to hide a car was in a bunch of cars. He knew that. But to him it was ballooning into a monolith with flashing neons, saying "Here I am. How can you miss me?"

The motel owner had walked out of his office, was standing in the drive, lighting a cigarette, looking. What the hell was he looking at? The traffic on the highway, the sky, up and down the gravel. Didn't he have anything better to do—or was he looking for a purpose?

Slit reached back, grabbed his brushed pants, pulled them on. Benny Hill's elfin insanities held no interest for him now; he never took his eyes from the man in the drive.

Now there was a local cop car cruising up the drive.

Slit yanked on his jacket, wincing at the rasp of harsh cloth over scratches, slipped out of his door and into the shadows of the ice and soda arcade. The motel owner never saw him, and the cop car was too far away. He waited, hardly breathing, behind the side of the soda machine.

The car slowed up, a cheerful voice called, "Evenin'. Any problems?"

"None I can't handle." The motel owner ground his butt beneath his foot. "They found that guy yet?"

"No, and they probably won't. For my money he's long gone. You know these young fellows with all the new gadgets—they get to thinkin' they're real heavy metal in the police business. Lots of luck, I say. Light crowd tonight?" The local cop's eyes swept the parked cars.

"Very light. Middle of the week."

"Nice looking Trans Am. Well, better get rolling. I'll be back about midnight."

"Okay. 'Night."

" 'Night."

The car left. The operator went back in. Slit let out his breath. Torn between contempt and irritation, he returned to his room, peeled off his jacket again, and cursed at the blood oozing from freshly opened scratches.

"Benny Hill" was over, but he found an old movie.

He didn't sleep at all.

Four o'clock found him swinging long legs to the carpet, tiptoeing back to the drapes. There'd been a sound of feet outside.

The guy next door was going quietly, almost surreptitiously, to the Trans Am. He got in, closed the door, drove away.

He did not, Slit also noticed, head into town, but went out toward the highway. Slit grinned. The little lady next door was in for a surprise when she woke up.

Served her right. Served them all right.

Was Mona asleep? Or was she cringing at every car that drove their street, at every footfall?

Let her cringe. She was having a picnic compared to what it was going to be like when he got home.

And she knew it. That was the good thing; she *knew*.

He laid back down on the rumpled bed, but he couldn't sleep. He kept seeing images on the ceiling. Some he liked. Some he didn't.

He'd done enough of that earlier.

One thing was always guaranteed to soothe him. He swung

bare legs to the floor again, took his knife from its sheath and and a worn whetstone from the pocket of his pants. He began to sharpen, and the fine rasp was almost like a song . . .

The blade was getting thinner. He looked at it sadly. He hated to see old friends wear out.

When it was safely back in its holder, he reached to his pants again. The right seam on the outside of his thigh was a little thicker. Not much. Not noticeably. He put his fingers on a round metal head not any larger than a corsage pin and drew forth his auxiliary weapon—the vicious, tiny stiletto that in his private thoughts he referred to affectionately as ''the kid.'' He put his fingertip on the end. Even with such light pressure it pricked and drew blood. It would go into a man like butter. He knew. It had.

It probably would again.

Chapter Fourteen

WILL'S SLEEP THAT night was like a bad piece of movie film, flickering on and off, on and off. He waked at everything —Bowser making slurp-slurp noises at his water bowl, the measured bong-bong of Grandmother Westerson's old eight-day clock, the squeak of his own bed as he thrashed around trying to get comfortable.

At one time his eyes popped wide open in the dark, and he said aloud, "Brachetti! Sure. A little guy. Cooked the books for some construction outfit once and did time. After that, he hung around the tracks across the river. Who'd want to waste him?"

He drifted back to sleep wondering why a penny-ante bookie could be important enough to merit the attentions of a high-priced hit man like Slit.

Then it was Slit in his dreams, or rather, the shadow of Slit, because they'd never been able to be certain of the man although they recognized his work. Its hallmark was neatness. Dispatch. A cold, heartless efficiency that made you wonder about the man responsible, wonder if he felt anything, if he cared for anybody.

If the man he'd seen had been Slit. If. If.

This time he drifted into a wild, disordered sort of dream, of shadowy, large men with knives, and then of Linda in danger.

In that instant Will woke up and twisted half off his bed, his body sheltering his pillow. The old dog, Bowser, nosed him in alarm, and daylight streamed through dirty windowpanes across his rumpled bed.

For one moment he could only lay still, gasping, cold, trying to sort out the mess in his whirling head.

Then he had, at last, what his mind had been trying to tell him for hours, and he said, "Oh my God!"

He scrambled up, stubbed his toe on the dresser, howled, staggered into the dining room, and grabbed the telephone on the wall.

He knew the voice that answered: one of the deputies. He said, "Will Westerson. Where did they find Linda Pietra's glasses?"

"What?"

He swallowed his gall. He made himself repeat clearly, "Linda Pietra's glasses. Where were they found?"

"Oh. Yeah. Wait a minute."

Clenching his teeth, Will waited, hearing in the background the familiar voices, clatter, and hustle of a police station. Then the deputy came back. "Will?"

"Here."

"In Charley Jackson's pasture. She'd called him, and he was looking for them when he found our body."

Will groaned. His worst fears were realized. Now he knew why the silent man in the Ford had stayed around. Now he knew, if there was to be a second body, whose body it would be.

He must have thought she'd seen him. He couldn't know that Linda without her glasses was as blind as a bat.

It had been Linda he'd been stalking! Linda! At the Bellam's, and—

There *had* been someone in his lane—and he'd told her it was a fence post!

Six o'clock. Almost six-thirty. Ten hours since he'd seen Linda alive!

Scarcely five minutes later, he was bouncing down his rutted driveway in his pickup truck. She didn't answer the phone in her apartment. The police were already on their way there. But she could have gone to the airport as she did every morning.

The airport was closest to him; he was going there first. Praying.

If she wasn't there . . .

He turned out on the highway. The sun was shining, and it was a beautiful morning. He put his foot down clear to the floorboards.

Chapter Fifteen

LINDA PIETRA WAS not at her best as she drove to the airport that early morning.

In the small favors department, Tony had been gone when she'd entered her apartment at five-thirty. She'd hardly slept, and Sue's narrow couch had nothing to do with it. Her mind had been like a bubbling pot, with the bubbles popping before she could grasp at their meaning yet leaving a circle of hurt, of anxiety. And when she'd finally gone to sleep, her dreams had been frightening, full of shadows and edged with unknown terror.

She stood in her shower, face raised to the sharp hot needles, trying to wash away the nagging sense that something was attempting to capture her attention, to point out some terribly important factor that she, in her distress, had utterly missed.

But, about what? Will? No way. There was nothing she'd missed during the long night in thinking about Will. She'd bombed, she'd goofed, she'd made a monumental fool of herself, and, in so doing, had humiliated them both—and that would be stuck in both their craws for a long, long time.

As she dressed, she snapped the radio on and vaguely heard something about a local excitement, a body being found. But deer season was on, bodies were always being found in deer season, and she paid little attention. She did wonder in a fleeting fashion if Ron's roadblock had been successful, but there was no obvious connection between that and the radio report and she made none on her own.

Trying to bolster her ego she pulled on new corduroy slacks, sucked in her stomach as she zipped them closed, and eyed herself critically sideways. Not too bad, but she'd better go easy on the jelly doughnuts for a while. The blouse matching the pants was old-fashioned with ruffles and lace. On top of it she pulled on a ratty sweatshirt with a faded Western Illinois logo on the front—sort of a downer for a new outfit, but it was going to be cold flying the Cub.

Would Mr. Black show up? She more than half hoped not. She'd called her dad late last night, and he'd reacted like a wounded moose. In the first place, he needed and was counting on his daughter doing the Cub act at the air show; in the second place, why did she want to sell it, anyway? Any Tootsie, he said querulously, in tight pants looked good getting out of a Pitt, but to look good getting out of a Cub took class—for which piggy remark she'd hung up on him.

He and Will didn't know each other, but they'd obviously hit it off if they met.

Now, in the bright early morning, she went into the kitchen, frowned at the dirty dishes, and shook a clenched fist at an absent Tony. She ought to mail them to him; by the time he got in from that Cairo run, they ought to be good and moldy!

But she'd never do it. She was too easy.

She said the agricultural word again and, scowling, got out the wetting solution for her contacts. Today was not the day to take a chance on losing her last pair of glasses.

Tying a bandanna around her head, she found the coffee stone-cold in her cup, abandoned it, picked up her Cub keys, and left.

It was a beautiful morning. The sky was sapphire, the sun crisply burning off the last patches of mist in the hollows. Clumps of goldenrod and chicory touched the fading green of the roadside with yellow and blue. Hawks were wheeling overhead, shaking last night's damp kinks from graceful wings.

She should have felt fine. She didn't. She felt awful.

She drove up the airport road and parked her car at the fence. Three other cars were lined up empty and locked; other than that, the place was sound asleep. Getting out of her

Chevy, she avoided glancing across Will Westerson's shorn, brown bean fields. But she knew where his house was—in that timbered dip beyond. Was there a thin thread of smoke trailing upward? Was that damned blonde pouring his coffee, smiling at him?

Stop it! said Linda to herself sharply, angrily. *There's no good in thinking such things. They are negative thoughts, destructive, sadistic!*

She pushed open the steel gate with its customary squeak and went reluctantly across the damp, deserted taxiway, avoiding the puddles and automatically patting the handsome old T-34 trainer plane as she went by.

It was five after six.

I'll wait until six-thirty, she promised herself. *Then if he hasn't shown up, I'll forget it and go on. I can use the extra half hour on my aileron rolls: . . .*

Beyond the tails of the Cub and the Stinson, on the faraway stretch of the concrete runway, a deer was poised in the early sun, its head stretched, sensing the wind, its white tail flicking. As she looked, it turned and trotted with unhurried grace across the concrete and down into the trees.

Following it with her eyes, suddenly—like a dash of cold water—Linda found herself staring into the black sunglasses of a very tall man standing on the other side of the Cub.

She was instantly aware of being chilled.

But why?

Because he came. Because that must be Mr. Black and she hadn't wanted him to come, but he had. And now she had to share her morning with him—and her airplane.

She put a cardboard smile on her face and kept putting one foot before the other. He didn't move, only swiveled as she came around the nose of the Cub to meet him.

He was large. He wore a zipped-up windbreaker with his hands thrust into slash pockets, and those sunglasses, in some indefinable way, rendered the iron-hard planes of his face almost statuelike. He said, softly, "Linda? Good morning."

He held out a gloved hand.

She answered, "Yes. Good morning."

Her own hand was tangled in the baggy pocket of her sweat-shirt. As she struggled to get it out, the sput-sput of a cold motorcycle sounded across the concrete. Tommy, arriving at work, drove his small Honda in a wide parabola toward them, waving. He called, cheerfully, "Hi! You're early!" and glanced curiously at Mr. Black's bent back as he picked a crumpled cigarette pack from the runway.

Linda replied, "I have a lot to do."

She couldn't see Slit's face, and the expression of balked anger had been carefully erased as the nosy kid went on to park his bike and he faced her again.

Scratch Plan One. No neat, soundless attack and a casual walk back to his car leaving a dead girl screened from view inside her own airplane.

So, Plan Two. Get her to give him a demo ride to some other airport, preferably a busy one where they'd go unnoticed. *Then* walk away, leaving behind the same dead girl. Having no car was no problem. He'd find a car.

He looked her squarely in the face, searching for some sign of recognition. There was none. They shook hands at last—a great deal less lethally then he'd planned. He said affably, "I really appreciate your coming out this early."

She answered, "I usually come out and fly every morning when I can." Then she took a deep breath. "What would you like to know about the Cub?"

Why did she feel those eyes behind the black lenses were boring into her? He smiled, showing square white teeth, and for some dumb reason the line ran through her mind, "The better to eat you with." But all he said was a mild, "Remember, I'm not a pilot. Whatever my son should know."

He certainly sounded harmless enough. Why was she so jumpy? She made herself answer. "Okay. This is a prewar 1940 Piper J-3, in the original yellow, with wheelpants. That's sort of rare. It probably gives me a few more miles per hour—which, believe me, in a Cub, still doesn't win any races.'' She smiled weakly; he did not. She went on, ''It's powered by a sixty-five horsepower Continental engine; there's twenty hours on the major, and it's been recently annualed. I have all the logbooks up to date—and I'm not certain I want to sell. You may be wasting your time.''

The last came in a rush.

He put the notebook he'd been writing in back in his pocket and answered softly, ''I think not. May I see inside?''

''Oh. Of course.''

He followed her around the nose and suddenly realized that this was a very different sort of aircraft than he'd ever been close to. It was not hard and shiny and substantial. The body was too skinny. There were black things on either side of the propeller that made it look like some giant yellow grasshopper. From a science fiction movie in which bugs took over the world. And 1940—that was almost fifty years ago! Personally, he wouldn't buy this thing with a wooden nickel.

But it flew. He'd seen it. And it must be safe—this broad didn't look like the daredevil type.

She was opening the door; standing by her, he received another shock. He inadvertently touched the yellow side. And it gave!

Seeing his startled look, she said briefly, ''Rag.'' Then she corrected herself: ''Fabric. You didn't know that?''

''No.'' And despite himself, he felt a small queasy sensation in the pit of his stomach—a warning going off, telling him he was getting out of his depth, too far away from an environment he could control.

But he'd never known failure before—especially at the hands of a broad. It stung. Even aware that if Westerson had nailed him and that it was only a matter of time before they all came looking—even then—he wouldn't cut his losses.

He was not about to be bested by a broad.

The door was in two halves. She stuck the window half up and secured it to a latch beneath the wing. The bottom half flopped down. She said to him, "There you are. Pretty basic. Altimeter, oil, compass. That's the throttle on the left side, under the window. And the sticks. I usually fly from the back when I'm by myself. This is an old Cub, so she has heel brakes that work—" and she suddenly grinned, "most of the time. That piece of wire sticking up from the nose is the gas gauge. When you can't see the wire you're out of gas. The tank holds almost twelve actual gallons of eighty octane, if you squeeze."

It reminded him of an old Model A Ford his grandpa had owned in the thirties. The thought comforted him. An eight-year-old kid could drive a Model A.

Something was missing. He frowned. "Where's the radio?"

She grinned again. "No radio. Look, it may come as a surprise, but you don't fall out of the sky without a radio. Trust me."

He certainly didn't mind the absence of communication. That part worked right into his hands. But he didn't enjoy the suspicion that for some reason she was more amused than she showed. He'd never liked being laughed at. A bit stiffly he asked, "How do you take off or land?"

"You let a controlled field know you're coming by telephone, and when you show, they give you a green light. Or you land on roads, football fields, or cow pastures. Cubby's aren't particular. My dad took one into a hayfield once and borrowed three gallons of tractor gas from a guy plowing his garden."

A light went on inside Slit's head. Carefully he asked, "You're serious?" because if she were, he'd just gotten a fantastic solution to his problem.

She shrugged. "Totally. Do you have a hayfield you want to land in?"

Come into my parlor said the spider to the fly. He almost said it aloud because, bingo, everything was snapping into place!

His favorite spot! He'd never gotten there with Joey. Joey had taken fright a few miles short and bolted. But it was still there. Waiting, quiet and deserted, since the narcs had busted the nice little drug trade going in and out of there two weeks ago.

Slit knew it well. There was a rundown house smack on top
the river bluff, flanked by two or three shacky buildings—one
of them with a pickup truck inside. No keys, but Slit knew
where they were hidden, and since the owner was occupied
elsewhere in government accommodations, he wasn't in a
position to complain. Best of all was the landing strip next to
the house—nicely mowed by said absent owner and made to
order for this job.

Slit felt good. He hadn't felt so good in two days.

"I might think of one," he said casually. "Would you take
me up? I'll buy your gas, of course."

She answered, "Sure," and tried not to let it sound reluc-
tant.

She sent him to untie the tail while she did her preflight.
Beneath the belly of the old Stinson, he glimpsed another car
pulling into the parking area, a guy with a briefcase getting out.
More people.

So there was no going back. This was it.

The round-faced little snip in the sweatshirt had reached in
and taken out the stick in the back. She lifted a locker lid
behind the seat and dropped it in. "You'll need the room,"
she told him. "Now. Believe me—there's no graceful way to
get into a Cub. Throw your left foot in and lift yourself up. And
if you put a foot through my gear leg, I'll break yours. It's
fabric and not a step. Heave!"

He heaved and found himself in the narrow sling seat, with
his knees stuck up before him like oversized chicken wings. "I
hope your son is shorter," she said, and leaned in over his lap.
He caught his breath and made a lightning assessment. The
back of her bandannaed head and her shoulders were defenseless . . .

Then a cheery voice said, "Hey, Linda, need a prop job?"

It was the guy with the briefcase.

Linda said, "Hi, Mr. Kitchel. I'd appreciate it. Hang on."

She had reached over, found the other half of the seat belt,
and fastened the two together so tightly it almost cut him in

two. Dismayed, he'd ducked his head down, but the guy with the briefcase never even looked. He went out of sight around the high nose of the Cub.

"Here," Linda said to Slit, and crossed his feet at the ankles. "That's to keep you off the control cables along the side. Okay. We're set. Sit tight."

She tossed something else into the locker behind his head —the "For Sale" sign. Then popping her round fanny into the seat ahead of him, she fastened her own belt, reached up, and stuck a key in the switch above her.

Linda craned her neck to look at the wind tee. From the south and pretty steady. She'd take off from the north end of the runway. "Pull her through a couple of times, will you, Mr. Kitchel?"

An unseen voice said, "Glad to."

The airplane shook a little, making sucking noises. Then Linda said, "Okay. Brakes on. Throttle cracked. Give her a shot."

Slit saw a hand appear and grasp the propeller tip. A leg in gray flannel came up. The prop went down and around in jumps. Then stopped. Was that how this junk heap was supposed to start? Why the hell couldn't the broad own a real airplane?

Linda was saying calmly. "She's cold. Try again."

"Should I pull her through some more?"

"I don't think so. I flew her yesterday. She's just chilly. Okay. Throttle cracked. Brakes on."

This time the engine sputtered. Caught. Died.

Linda said her dirty word. "Sorry. One more time. Brakes on. Throttle cracked."

The Continental caught, the prop disappeared into a whirling arc. Linda waved her hand, mouthed, "Thanks!"

They began to move.

As Slit's first anxiety resolved into relief, he noticed something else—the window was still up and the door down. The idiot woman—she had the brains of an ant; he'd have thought the FAA had more sense than to let a dumb broad like this have a license!

He tapped her on the shoulder, pointed.

She nodded, but went right on steering the plane around the bend of the taxiway onto the long, level concrete runway, then across the runway and onto the grass! She couldn't even keep it on the road!

What the hell was he doing here? He had to have been out of his mind. There must have been another way . . .

She was swinging the long tail around, fanning the grass. The engine roared.

His hands went to his seat buckle in a panic. He had to get out of this thing. There were trees on his left and a gully; he could make it to there. Then he'd figure out something else . . .

Too late. They were moving, bouncing, gaining speed. In the air! Good God, not a hundred yards and they were in the air and the door was still open.

Wind rushed across his knees, the roaring engine filled his ears, and beneath him the land was dropping away, turning to toy houses, miniature cars . . .

Up front, Linda watched her altimeter, leveled off, and began her turn. She was thinking, *This is going to be short. I don't like that man. I don't know why. But I don't. And he's not going to buy my Cub.*

Around the patch. That's what they'd do. Then land, and she'd get rid of him. It was too beautiful a morning to ruin.

She was glad she'd left the door down. Maybe she could freeze him out. She grinned to herself.

Behind her, Slit was not grinning, but he was recovering his cool. The air was smooth, and the engine was now making a calm, reassuring thrum. It was colder than hell with the stupid door open, but he could hack that. For a while, anyway.

She was turning the thing. He looked down again, past his feet, and saw tiny cows, the blue of a lake, then the airport parking lot with a baby pickup truck wheeling in off the ribbon-sized highway. And something else.

Two black-and-whites, with red lights flashing! And they were turning into the airport too!

She was looking, too. He could see her profile, frowning. Wondering. Time to move.

He unsnapped his belt and leaned forward. In one swift movement the point of his knife touched her ribs.

Chapter Sixteen

"OKAY, LINDA," HE said in her ear. "This is a very pointed knife. I keep it that way. You don't want to know why. Stay calm. Do as I say. Then it won't hurt you."

Linda only caught part of what he said over the roar of the engine. But she felt the knife through her sweatshirt and her blouse. Her first reaction was sheer disbelief.

But the knife blade was real. She knew it was real as he pushed a little harder.

She reached over, throttled back.

The noise diminished but the knife jabbed. He said harshly, "Why did you do that?"

"So I can hear! Have you gone crazy? What do you want?"

"Go west. Toward the river."

"We are going west. But look—whoever you are—if I'm being hijacked, you have the wrong plane! With hardly twelve gallons of fuel at fifty-five miles an hour in this wind . . ."

A gust of morning wind hit them; the plane bounced; the engine roared; he grabbed on and yelled, "Don't do that!"

"I didn't. The wind did. Where are we going?"

"Never mind. Just listen to me. Do exactly what I say. And don't try anything funny."

And don't try anything funny!

Right out of a Grade-B movie!

I don't believe this, she thought incredulously. *The guy is nuts. He's cracked up!*

Then she realized that he was why the police had been pouring into the airport. They were looking for him! He wasn't a dip.

He was for real. But why her? Why the Cub? It made no sense! She swallowed. She shouted back, "Okay. Okay. We're heading west now. See, there's the river. What now?"

"Bear a shade south. Keep going."

She obeyed. Beneath them the square farm fields chugged by, the teeny pig houses, the grazing cows, the half-harvested bean fields. She could feel his breathing in her ear, and the knife jabbed again.

"Make this thing go faster!"

"I told you. With a headwind, fifty-five is about all we can do!"

They were over the river now. A towboat was moving upstream, pushing its grain barges along, leaving a creamy wake on the shining, lead-colored water. The bright rows of pleasure boats at the marina bobbed gracefully as the wash reached them. An early-morning boater was strolling the docks, leading a frolicking dot of a dog; he heard the engine, looked up, and waved.

In her ear the cold voice said, "I saw him, too. Don't make a move."

They were across the river now, over the little town. Her captor said, "South a hair more. Good. Good girl. Now listen nicely. There's a strip on the bluff. Do you know it?"

She nodded. Sure. Where they got the dope-runners a few weeks ago. God. Was that what he was? A hophead? She said loudly, "I've never landed there."

"You're going to now."

And if I do, I'm dead.

It was really that simple. Wasn't it? She knew about dope-runners. They didn't fool around, and they couldn't afford to be identified.

She had about five minutes. Five minutes. And he hadn't moved. The breath was still in her ear and the knife in her ribs.

Then one single fact struck her like a blow—he was leaning forward.

She knew how tightly he'd been belted in. She'd done it, herself.

He had unfastened his belt. He was sitting back there leaning forward. Off balance. And loose.

God, did she dare?

He said in her ear, "Just land this thing, sweetheart. Nice and easy. That's all you have to do."

She didn't believe it. She knew better.

Gradually she pulled, raising the nose, beginning an easy climb. Altitude. She needed altitude. . . .

When she was high enough, she shoved the throttle forward, kicked hard right rudder, pulled full right stick. The Cub went on its side, wing down. He yelled. She knew he'd grabbed the back of her seat, was holding on. The knife had disappeared, but she didn't know where. It could be out and gone, it could be still inside where he could reach it. She couldn't take a chance. He was screaming at her. She shoved the nose down, keeping the right rudder in. The air became centrifugal as they started spinning down. Down. Down . . .

He was cursing and screaming in her ear but hanging on tight. He was not falling out the door.

And she had to pull up. The ground was rising fast. She leveled off, shoved full power, nose down, stick back—the struts whined, creaked, *come on, baby, loop—loop—*

Around they went like the rim of a giant wheel, the earth circling with them. The sound of his voice changed; it garbled. He was retching; she smelled the sick, sweet smell of vomit, felt it wet her hair, gagged, but held on doggedly.

They were inverted, and his cry was pure, primitive terror. He was clinging with both hands and feet. But they couldn't stay inverted; the Cub would fuel-starve, sputter, quit. *Okay. Roll out of the loop—left rudder, left stick, right her, nose down, pull up. . . . Was that the wind screaming or the man in back? No matter, do it again. . . .*

It was him. He was begging, whimpering through his vomit, "Stop—stop—"

One more time, up we go and over the top—

Then she smelled something else.

Gas.

She pulled out and checked the fuel gauge. The wire on the nose was almost out of sight.

When she'd done the preflight, she must not have gotten the gascolator entirely closed. Cubs did that. She knew they did. She'd been careless. And they'd been leaking a fine thin stream of fuel ever since they took off.

It looked as if it was going to be the hilltop strip after all. She couldn't get back to Penfield.

Oh boy.

There it was, off to the right, running south—a browning scar cleaving the tops of the scrub fir.

Behind her, the man had the dry heaves. He even sounded as though he might be crying. But he had looked pretty healthy; he wouldn't be sick long. She had to hurry.

No circling this time, no pattern, no base leg. Just put her down and hope the wind hadn't changed. The south end of that strip dropped like a cliff face into a valley full of timber.

Linda took a deep breath. *Power back—watch the airspeed—trim. Back again, airspeed 40—okay, trim. Idle power, hold the stick as if there were no tomorrow—which there might not be.*

Flare. Touch. Roll.

And bounce. Bounce again! Come on, Cubby!

Down. Seesaw the heel brakes. Slowing. Slowing.

Stop. Cut the power. Grab the keys. Bail out.

Run.

Chapter Seventeen

THE YELLOW PLANE was already in the air.

As he'd come over the brow of the hill in his pickup truck, Will had seen it moving down the runway. By the time he'd turned in and slammed on his brakes at the fence, it was lifting into the air, nose up, and Jim Kitchel's Cessna was waiting its turn at the intersection. As he scrambled down and loped to the fence, the clear thrum of the Cub's Continental engine came to him through the crisp morning sunshine.

All he could do then was smash his doubled fist on the fence post and curse savagely through clenched teeth.

There was the old Ford, sitting empty.

Empty because he was with her.

Unless—

He wheeled on the lineboy coming up behind him. "Who's with Linda?"

Tommy blinked. "Who? I didn't know him. Tall guy with dark glasses. Hey, here comes Kitchel back—and listen to that engine! I'll bet his mag went. I told him. I told him last week . . ."

But Will was not interested in Jim Kitchel's engine problems. Nor, any longer, was Tom, because suddenly two police cars were screaming into the parking lot, red lights flashing. Guys spilled from them like blueberries from a bucket. Over Tom's bewildered, "What's going on?" one of the policemen shouted at Will, "She's not at the apartment!"

In answer, Will pointed upward.

All their eyes were glued on the yellow Cub, sailing slowly

out of sight in the blue ocean of a morning sky. Somebody asked, harshly, "Is he a pilot?"

Will answered, "I don't know. I have no idea." He clenched his teeth, hoping the guy wasn't. It might give Linda some sort of an edge. It might—if she knew she was in danger. But did she? Was she just innocently giving the guy a ride—a little morning pleasure? Except her generosity could only end one way. One way.

He closed his eyes, trying to get his frozen brains to work. One of the deputies said, "Radio! Can't we get her on the radio?"

"She hasn't got a radio."

"The guy out there on the runway—use him as a chase plane, have him radio back up to us . . ."

Will could tell, even if the police couldn't, that Kitchel in his Cessna was going nowhere. Not for some time. He shook his head, not even mentioning that aircraft and police bands were different anyway. She was flying west. West. What did that mean? Every morning he watched her flying west, over the river. Now he knew it was because she was practicing her aerobatics and needed unpopulated farm land beneath her. But she wouldn't be practicing aerobatics this morning—not with him on board. So where was she going? Where?

Kitchel had returned, wheeling his noisy Cessna up near the fence, holding his door open, yelling something that was drowned in his grating engine. Tom ran over, listened, jogged back as the Cessna went on, popping and spitting, toward the hangars. Tom said, "He says Linda's leaking gas. Her 'colator's not closed. She lost a puddle on the runway. He was going to try and catch her when his mag went. He says if we call Keith, he could probably take off in the Stinson and catch her before she runs out."

Keith lived in town. There was no time to call Keith.

Will felt bottomed out in despair. The police were standing around him, ground people all of them, standing like a circle of blue geese, looking at him, waiting for answers that only a pilot could give. They knew he was a pilot—except, God—he didn't have any answers! His girl had taken off in his Cub with an assassin, and he was as tied to the ground as they were!

He muttered, "An all-points! An all-points!"

The sheriff said, "Right!" Sliding into his car, he set his radios squawking as he put out the call for tabs on a yellow airplane flying west.

West out of sight. She was not even in view now if they squinted. West. Short of fuel. Quincy airport was too far north. There was Hannibal. Hull . . .

The sheriff yelled, "They have her in sight at the marina!"

The marina. That was south. Bowling Green. Vandalia. She'd notice the fuel shortage early on. She'd tell him. She'd tell him they had to land. Or else.

But where? The Cub could land in a feedlot, a pasture, a mountain valley . . .

Then it clicked! It finally clicked! His feet uprooted themselves, he yelled, "Hilltop!" and bolted for the sheriff's car.

It was already moving as he scrambled in. As it backed around, jerked into forward gear, and burned rubber down the driveway, the sheriff said tensely, "It gels. I hope to God you're right."

Behind Westerson's moustache his face was the color of clay. "They all know Hilltop," he said. *They* being the big, black shapeless mass of druggies and dealers and the empire behind them.

The sheriff nodded. He said, "If it's Hilltop, we'll need assistance." He was already on the horn, calling for it. They both knew they were ten minutes from the foot of the bluff and that the trail up took a four-wheel drive.

They screamed through town, shot past the highway fork and went southwest toward the river and Missouri. The speedometer was tapping ninety. It was slow.

The sheriff said, "She has no radios. Right?"

"Right."

"Then at least he's not listening to us."

"No. Just pray he isn't a pilot."

"Could he kill her in the air if he is a pilot?"

"Maybe." The one word ached with anguish. "She'd fly from the front seat. A single seat. He'd be behind her. If she left the back stick in and if he is a pilot—yeah. He could kill her. He'd just have to lean forward and she'd be dead. Then he could take the Cub over and fly it anywhere."

"Except he's short on gas."

"Right." He exhaled a gust of air that forced its way up his throat. "And if he knows about Cubs, he knows he doesn't have to land at Hilltop. He can put her down on a farm lane, a pasture, a side road . . .

"You're kidding." Then the sheriff regretted the words; they sounded asinine because Westerson obviously was not kidding. "It sounds to me as though you're right. We'd better pray he isn't a pilot. At least she'll have to be alive to bring it down. That's not buying a hell of a lot of time, but it's all we're likely to have." He touched the siren and nipped around a tractor pulling hay bales on a wagon. One of the guys across the river came blaring on the radio. Yeah, he could see a yellow airplane; it seemed to be climbing. He'd just come out of the coffee shop. "What the hell is going on?"

While he was told, they crossed the long Mississippi River bridge, ran the stoplights at the intersection that triangled the north edge of the little river town, and sped on around the bend into open country again. A Missouri patrol car had fallen in behind their two, and a four-wheel drive would be on the bluff road at about the same time they were.

Another report came in on the Cub. Its heading still seemed to be Hilltop—and it was also still climbing.

Climbing?

Will frowned. Why the hell was it climbing? The airstrip on the bluff was high but no mountaintop. It didn't need altitude; it had altitude. Why was the nose up?

He gritted his teeth, envisioning some sort of grim struggle going on inside his Cub, seeing it out of control, seeing it flut-tering like a big butterfly right smack into the side of a hill.

''There it is!''

The sheriff pointed through his windshield. ''About one o'clock—see it—a way up there.'' Then, ''Oh my God,'' and he almost took a tree.

Swerving in a magnificent arc back onto the highway again, he asked harshly, ''What's going on? What's happening?''

The yellow airplane—the size of a bright gold matchbox toy in the blue-paint sky—had suddenly turned precisely on its edge, wing pointing upward. Then, incredibly, the tail was up, both wings went horizontal, the nose dropped, and it began a smooth spiral directly downward. From a matchbox toy it became a spinning projectile, growing as it plunged.

Will's heart stuck. He muttered a curse, wanted to stop looking but couldn't.

The police car screeched to a stop as did the ones behind it. Everybody was hanging out the doors watching. In a sort of helpless frenzy, the sheriff was calling, ''What can I do? What can I do?'' over Will's hoarse voice as, not even aware he was yelling, he shouted, ''Pull her out! Damn you, pull her out. She's going in!''

No, she wasn't. Anyway, not right then. At what seemed to the gaping men below the very last possible minute, the yellow Cub raised her nose and went level with the ground.

Then, hardly giving them time to imagine the power struggle was over, the nose went up again, the airplane began to climb steadily, almost arching its slender back.

''Will,'' the sheriff said softly. ''What's it going to do now? It's on its back! Will, is *anybody* flying that thing? It's coming down again—look at it come . . . ''

Loop, Will was saying silently. *Loop, damn you! If you loop, then I'll know! I'll know what's going on!*

It looped. It went entirely under, started to climb, went in-verted again, and he was answering the sheriff's anguished question about whether anyone was flying it, saying, "Yes, somebody's flying that Cub—a hell of a good pilot, that's who's flying it!"

"Then what in God's name does he think he's doing?"

"She! That's Linda up there—I know that's Linda! And she's either trying to shake the guy out or scare him to death! Come on!"

"They're still upside down!"

"Not for long. It'll quit, and she knows it! See—there they go over. Now she has to land, she has to be near tapping empty."

They were already moving. The sheriff asked, "Where? Still Hilltop?"

Will was craning his neck through the window, watching. "Yeah, Hilltop. It has to be Hilltop. It's the nearest place now. The valley's too full of timber and the highway's too busy."

The sheriff groaned. "Have you been up there?"

"No. Never."

"That trail's for billy goats!" Then, at the fear on Westerson's face, he added, "We'll do what we can, man! We'll be billy goats!"

The airplane had gone out of sight because they were in the shadow of the bluff itself. Two four-wheel drive Jeeps were idling at the intersection. They scrambled out of the county cars and piled into the Jeeps. The Jeeps lurched into gear and started upward.

Hanging on, Will asked, "Doesn't anyone live there?"

"On top? Wild turkeys and a few deer. The guy who owned the place is doing time—watch those rocks!" The informative voice suddenly ended in panic as everyone grabbed on, the vehicle careened perilously close to the rim of the road, and three loose pieces of limestone bounced on down into the valley.

That stretch, however, was easy, compared to the rest. The road angled, became a lane, then a wagon trail. It made another ninety-degree turn with the outside dropping off into a rockfall and the inside scraping barberry bushes. Then it went straight up.

The driver shifted down as far as he could. The Jeep labored, rolling loose scree back of its wheels, spraying it at the windshield of the one behind.

They'd never make it. Never. They'd be too late. The Cub was down by now. Linda was alone up there with that snake. She hadn't a chance.

The sheriff was feeling it, too. "Enough of this noise," he muttered, and bailed out.

Will was right on his heels with the rest of them behind him.

"This way," the sheriff said. "Right, Len? You've hunted up here."

"Right. That way a big ravine cuts you off. Work up and left."

Will was already scrambling.

The sheriff called, "Westerson!"

Will paused, caught the handgun, stuck it in his belt, reached out for a handful of sumac, and pulled himself up the bank through moss and ooze. Behind him, he heard the Jeeps grunt, spin, move on.

On top of the sumac bank was a rusty, limping fence, then a narrow field, patched with goldenrod and full of groundhog burrows, then a band of loose, limestone shelving. Will's heart began to pound. His legs ached. Behind him he could hear others rasping for breath.

But that's all he could hear.

No airplane. No voices.

Damn.

They couldn't have been wrong.

No. Him. He'd made the decision. He was the pilot; he had said "Hilltop." What if he'd been wrong? What if they broke out into the clearing and it was empty?

For what if there was one small, limp body by a yellow Cub? Which would be worse?

A blackberry bramble caught at his pants leg, penetrated, ripped his knee with tiny knives, then curled around the other foot, almost tripping him. A rabbit shot out right beneath his hand and bounded away in great leaps. A squirrel scolded above him.

Another sagging fence.

He staggered over it, almost catching the sheriff in the teeth with his shoe. The sheriff grabbed at his jacket tail.

"Hang on."

"What?"

"I said, 'hang on'! The runway is right up there—on the other side of those cottonwood trees."

"Okay. It's your show. What next?"

"Let's have a look. Easy."

Will followed him through the scrub trees, avoiding the dead, crackling brush. He caught a glimpse of yellow and his heart jumped.

It was there. The Cub was there.

So it was. Sitting quietly. Still trickling a thin drip of fuel.

But Linda wasn't.

Nor was the man called Slit.

Chapter Eighteen

THE MAN CALLED Slit had never been in such pain. In his miserable retching, the top of his stomach had jammed itself up through the split in his diaphragm; the torn diaphragm had tensed, trapping the stomach top like a wire around a bag, and he was immobilized, rigid with agony.

Thank God, the broad didn't know. She could have taken him, then, as easily as a week-old baby. Instead, she bailed out and bolted. From the corners of his eyes, he could see her scrambling for the brush at the edge of the field. But he couldn't move. Not yet. Not until the waves of pain subsided, not until that diaphragm muscle relaxed, dropped the stomach back, and actually not even then. The whole thing wrung him out, left him weak as water. It would take him five, ten minutes to get back to normal.

At least he knew the terrain. She didn't. She wouldn't get very far.

Linda knew only one thing: She needed cover, and she needed it fast.

It wouldn't be long before he'd come after her.

And she was all alone. She had nothing but her wits--and not too many of them. The fact that she'd been a gullible fool was something to kick herself about later. Right now the name of the game was survival.

There were some shacks on a dogleg to her right, along the edge of the runway. The highway was on the left, down there below, somewhere. But the nearest cover was on the right.

She scrambled out and sprinted for it, dashed in among the brambles, lost her footing, and rolled bruisingly down a muddy water seep. She came to a stop against a mossy sycamore stump with a thump. Birds exploded from the foliage above as if shot from a gun. But there was no noise from the runway. Not yet.

She got to her knees, crept cautiously through heavy leaf mold to the cover of a wild-plum thicket. Then cautiously, cautiously, she edged her way higher until she could glimpse the yellow Cub through the tangled brush.

The Cub was on her left, now.

Panting painfully in short, dry gasps, she pushed at the leafless bushes, scratching her hands as she tried to clear a view. She had to know where he was.

She knew what he wanted to do.

She couldn't imagine why. Why her? What had she done?

But it didn't matter. It didn't matter at all.

What mattered was that he was crazy, and he'd kill her immediately if he got another chance.

The old sweatshirt caught on thorns and snagged as she pulled it free. The twitch loosened scree beneath her feet and she started to slide again. She grabbed at the bushes, scrabbled with her toes, and found another footing.

Hanging on, she peered through brush at the Cub. Her heart almost stopped beating as she saw the man, standing by the plane's nose. He was wiping his mouth with the back of his hand. His dark glasses were gone. Hair clung in sticky wet points on his forehead, and the look of rage on his cheese-colored face was savage.

Like a cornered rabbit, she watched him as he turned his head slowly like a snake. He looked right at her.

But he didn't see her. It took a moment to realize that. He didn't see her. He was just—looking.

He also looked at the weather-beaten buildings down at the other end, at the beginning of the runway where she'd brought the Cub in over the trees, and at the ridge on the left where,

beyond wild grape and cottonwood the road curved down toward the highway.

Something seemed to be wrong with one hand. He was
licking it with his tongue, like an animal licks a hurt, while all
time hung suspended beneath the blue morning sky.

He turned up his jacket collar. He was still cold. Then he
reached back into the airplane. She saw what he got, what he
held in his hand: his knife.

He stepped back and raised the knife. She almost cried out.
But she couldn't. She knew she couldn't. She could only
huddle in abject misery, tears running down her cheeks, as he
plunged his knife again and again into the Cub's sleek sides and
the graceful wing, ripping and slashing the fabric with savage
pleasure.

She thought he'd never stop. But he did. Finally. He put the
knife away. Carefully. Then he raised one big foot and brought
it smashing down through the right gear leg. He was smiling.

She hid her head in her hands, shaking, unable to watch
anymore.

But apparently that had vented his spleen. When she looked
again, he was almost at the edge of the runway on the opposite
side.

The highway side.

He was giving up, going to the highway.

He wasn't going to look for her!

Still, native caution prevailed. She watched until he was com-
pletely out of sight, and even then, didn't show herself in the
clear. She edged her way through the brush south along the rim
of the dogleg, going toward the old buildings. Maybe there was
someone there. At least a phone. She knew there was elec-
tricity; she could see the poles. At least she'd find somewhere
to hide. She wasn't going down on that road. Not for a long,
long time. Give her credit for some smarts.

They had to come looking. Someone would! Someone would
see her poor baby sitting there in tatters, someone at the airport

would miss her, realize she'd not come back, put two and two together.

All she had to do was hole up and wait.

She was close to the buildings now. Everything was quiet. The tattered pink shreds of a once-orange windsock swung idly on its wire frame above a sagging open shed, piled with trash and overgrown with berry bushes. On the weathered front of another building a gray door sagged half open. From it came a moldy smell of damp earth. There was also the muted gleam of metal. Headlights.

A truck. An old pickup truck!

She looked around. Nothing moved. Nothing was in sight. She took a deep breath, broke from her cover, ran across the narrow strip of browning turf, and put her hand on the sagging door.

Then behind her a cold voice said, "I thought you'd come here."

She whirled, terrified.

There he was, a few feet away. Smiling.

She knew immediately she'd been tricked. He hadn't gone to the highway. He'd followed the road around to these buildings, keeping out of sight, waiting for her.

And she had fallen for it.

She screamed.

She ran, as Joey Brachetti had run.

But Linda was, in a way, luckier. She stumbled on the rough tussocks, and the knife sung over her head, burying itself harmlessly into the runway. She staggered up, ran on, no longer screaming, saving her breath as she heard his long legs pounding the turf behind her, cursing her, calling her filthy names.

Then two things happened. A voice shouted, "Freeze!" and a shot rang out.

The man behind her stiffened, threw up his arms, and pitched forward.

But Linda didn't see. She ran on, mindlessly, sobbing, almost blindly. There were still feet behind her, coming closer. She could hear them!

A hand closed on her arm. She jerked away in terror, stumbled, was caught, and screamed.

But the arms held her tightly, and a voice was saying her name over and over again: "Linda! Linda!"

She stopped and opened her eyes. A face danced before her, a face she didn't believe—a brown face, dark-browed, dark-moustached beneath a greasy Massey Ferguson red cap. She gulped. She whimpered, "Will?" then went into a heap in his arms. A warm, muddy, tattered, smelly heap. But alive. Very alive.

Behind them an angry, thunder-browed sheriff was kneeling over a fallen man. He was barking, "I told you to hold your fire! Who the hell squeezed off that shot?"

A calm voice answered, "You didn't tell me."

He looked up into the dark eyes of a heavily muscled stranger in city clothes. "Who the hell are you?"

"Steve Staszewski. St. Louis." The guy was holding out his shiny badge. "I joined up down the road a piece. I'm supposed to take this joker back in my custody—now that you've got him. The papers are on their way. I suppose I've got ahead of them."

"Yeah." The word said absolutely nothing. But the sheriff's eyes flicked to his peers. They caught the glance. Something not kosher here.

"Offhand," the sheriff went on slowly, "I'd say he'd better go back to town and get this bleeding taken care of. Did they," and there was the barest accent on the word 'they,' "tell you to bring him back dead?"

"Damn it, sheriff, I thought he was going to nail the girl!"

The deputy kneeling on the other side said, "He'll be okay. It just nicked him."

The sheriff climbed to his feet, brushing dead leaves from his knees. His eyes were very noncommittal. "Let's get him patched up. Then we'll talk about custody."

Steve Staszewsky had a struggle keeping his face bland. Stupid country cop!

Oh, well. Go along with the rube. Don't make waves. There would be a chance. Somewhere. Accidents happen all the time—when well staged. He knew. He'd staged a couple.

Suddenly, from the ground, Slit's eyes opened. They looked squarely up at Staszewsky. They were a cold, unblinking gray. Despite himself, Straszewsky felt a chill.

But he couldn't know. He couldn't! Even if he suspected a contract out on him, he'd not connect it with a cop! So the guy just looked mean because he was mean. Like a trapped cobra.

From the comfort of Will's supporting arms, Linda was still trying to figure out why all these bad things had happened to her and her Cub, when one of the policemen discovered the roll of film that had fallen out of Slit's pocket.

"Hey, that's my roll of film!" Linda was even more puzzled than before. "I mean it's Vivian's. She gave it to me and I gave it to Ron to drop off at the drugstore. I know it's the same film—Viv put her initials on it with a marker. See? V. E."

"What's on the film?"

Bewildered, she answered, "Nothing. That is, nothing important." She thought a moment. "Just Viv's grandson, Jeffy. Jeffy and his first birthday cake."

A low groan came from the figure on the ground. Mistaking Slit's fury for pain, the sheriff began marshalling his forces again. "Len. You and Bill. This character's beginning to hurt. Let's get him moved before he sues us for neglect." He pointedly ignored the stocky policeman from St. Louis.

One of the Missouri men was coming toward them with Slit's knife, carrying it carefully where the haft joined the blade. "Some pig sticker, huh."

Will answered grimly, "He's very good with those. He hasn't, by any chance, got another one, has he?" Will was careful to avoid even the suggestion that they might not have searched the creep. Wouldn't be politic.

"No. We checked. He's clean."

The two deputies had hoisted Slit to his feet. He shook them off imperiously and stood by himself. He was holding a bloody handkerchief to his ribs. His eyes were still fixed on Staszewsky. And it was making Staszewsky nervous, the sheriff noticed. Staszewsky asked, ''Aren't you going to cuff him?'' There was no tact at all in his phrasing; the question was obviously a rebuke.

One of the dupties bristled, ''Why? He's not going any-where.''

Looking around for support, Steve noticed Will for the first time and seemed surprised. ''Hello, Lieutenant.''

Will ignored the use of his former title. He nodded, ''Did Elman send you?''

But Will didn't hear his answer, for Linda had suddenly turned ashen and slumped against him, making a soft, pitiful sound in her throat.

She had been looking at the deep striations on Slit's bared chest—they'd started to bleed again—and had thought that they looked like they might have been made by a cat. . . .

And then her knees had turned to water.

Pussycat. His mouse. In the closet.

That hullabaloo in the foyer with the stray dog!

Her creepy, crawly sense of being watched.

And—oh, no—the man in Will's lane!

Then it hadn't been a fluke or her imagination or a case of nerves! The man had been following her. Her! Not following —stalking. Stalking, as a wolf would stalk a rabbit.

''Why?'' she burst, staring into his cold gray eyes, eyes so frozen, so relentless without those black glasses. ''Why? Why me? I don't know you! What did I ever do that you'd want to hurt me?''

Will held her tighter, turned her away, held her face against his chest. Gently he said, ''He thought you'd seen him. When you flew over the pasture and lost your glasses.''

''But I can't see anything without my glasses!''

''He had no way of knowing that.''

Certain that she didn't want to hear the answer, she asked, ''What—what was he doing that I shouldn't have seen?''

''Killing a man.''

''With his knife? That knife?''

''With his knife, probably that one.''

Steve Staszewsky was getting impatient. He could stand almost anything better than being ignored. Especially by this bunch of rubes. ''Don't worry, lady,'' he interjected with a cheerfulness that seemed forced, ''I'm going to take him where he won't hurt anyone anymore.'' He felt very clever, smug even, at his double meaning. None of these idiots would get it.

But Slit understood. Suddenly he knew why Staszewsky was there.

The ice in his eyes ran downward, freezing him as it went, turning him to a statue. He felt as if he were dying. And he knew the raw truth—he was. He was dead as he stood.

There was no escape. Cops wouldn't help him. Screw the cops. No escape from the men who hired him—who would not tolerate failure.

He'd failed. Staszewsky had been sent to close the account. And if not Staszewsky, somebody else.

It was just a matter of time.

He'd better make the most of it.

Keeping his eyes on the muddy, disheveled broad with her torn pants, her blotchy, tear-streaked face and stinking hair —and not looking at the grinning Staszewsky—he reached down, rubbed his thigh, and winced.

One of the deputies laughed. ''Got banged around, didn't you, buddy? I don't mind saying, I'm glad it wasn't me up there getting turned upside down. You fly a pretty mean airplane, Ma'am.''

Linda's messy head jerked around.

The Cub! How could she forget the Cub, sitting over there in the clearing, shredded and tattered!

''Oh, Will,'' she said, and he nodded, answering quietly.

''Okay. We'll go have a quick look.''

"He took his knife to it! He was so mad at me, he took his knife to the Cub! And I didn't dare stop him!"

"Of course you didn't. And it can't be all that bad." He was trying to sound soothing.

She hiccoughed, and her face crumpled like a child about to cry. "He stomped the gear leg. I saw him. He stomped right through it!"

"Come on. We'll go check the damage. Right now." He called over her head to the sheriff, "We have to tie the airplane down. It shouldn't take too long."

"Sure. The boys have brought the Jeeps along the road to the buildings down there. Come on when you're through."

They'd walked about ten feet when Linda stumbled. Will stopped and looked at her squarely. "Have you got an eye problem?"

She nodded, feeling wretched. "One contact's gone into a corner."

"Hold still, then." He took her chin in one big hand and because she looked so touchingly vulnerable his voice was dry. "Good lord, you're a mess. I see the scamp. Hold still." He wet his fingertip, touched gently and gave her the tiny piece of plastic. "There we go. Don't drop it. Do you want the other out too? You look like you've been on a cheap drunk."

"I won't be able to see anything." Being told that she looked as awful as she knew she must made her sound truculent.

But for Will truculence was better than that hurt, terrified, and pitiful sound. He could handle truculence. "You don't need to see anything." He wrinkled his nose. "But you could use a shower. What did he do, chuck all over you when you turned him upside down?"

She hesitated. "Yes. When he stuck that knife in my ribs, I knew he'd unbuckled his seat belt because he was practically on top of my back." She took a steadying breath. "It was all I could think of to do."

"Don't apologize!" He sounded harsh. "I thought it was brilliant." Could she ever realize the terrible feeling he'd had watching her up in the sky, trying to get to the field, praying he'd guessed right and then seeing the airplane there—without her in it? Would he ever be able to tell her about that terrible feeling? He didn't know. A few minutes ago she'd come to his arms, clung to him. But she'd been scared. It didn't mean anything. How could it, after last night? He cleared his throat. "Let's have a look at the plane."

The wall had come up between them again. Linda could feel it. She could almost see it. It was a rude reminder that no matter what else had happened, nothing between them had really changed.

He took her arm to keep her from stumbling again and they set out across the brown uneven field toward the Cub.

Behind them, the sheriff and his entourage were nearing the two four-wheel drive vehicles, drawn up into the rutted neck of a driveway by the old buildings. Len and Bill flanked Slit, the sheriff walked behind them, and the rest of the men went before, the handsome dandy from St. Louis conspicuous among the blue uniforms and trooper hats.

Slit was limping. Suddenly he stumbled, pitching forward. Staszewsky and a trooper next to him staggered, unbalanced by the unexpected blow from behind. The trooper lost his hat.

"Damn it!" he snapped, dusting off his headgear. "Look where you're going and get in that Jeep!"

"Sorry," Slit said. He climbed into the back seat and sat, flanked by his two escorts. Bill was glancing back at the Cub, shaking his head.

"You sure did a number on that airplane, buddy."

Will was saying to Linda, "It's not so bad." Kneeling by the gear leg, he looked up at her. The wind ruffled his dark hair beneath the red cap and made little secret whisperings along the fading grass and the last few dandelions. The Cub was still cooling with small, tin noises. The wire sat on the nose, and her fuel was only a damp patch on the ground beneath.

He smiled up at her dirty, tragic face. "Don't feel so bad.

This old lady's been on hard times before. The gear will be a piece of cake. It's just damaged fabric; the frame's okay. You can patch that up, put a couple of rolls of duct tape on her fusilage and her wing, and fly her out of here.''

He didn't say a word about the half-closed fuel drain. This was not the time. Besides, he'd done the same thing once, and had to land on a county road. Instead, he hoisted himself to his feet, wiping his hands on his jacket. ''I just hope you know how to ribstitch. Got tie-downs?''

''In the locker.'' She nodded about the ribstitching. ''Dad taught me. We re-covered a Taylorcraft one winter.''

''This winter you re-cover a Cub. She's about due, anyway.''

He wasn't saying ''we.'' He was saying ''you.''

He took the steel anchors from her and screwed them into the ground, grunting, while she ran the ropes through the loops on the airplane. They were just finishing the tail when a sudden shout of alarm rose from the cluster of men by the Jeeps. It split the morning air, and four wild turkeys burst up from a cottonwood like flailing feather dusters.

Both Will and Linda spun around. ''What's that?'' she said.

''Something's wrong!'' He grabbed her hand. ''There's a guy on the ground. I can see him. It's not Slit. He's sitting in the Jeep. Come on!''

They hurried, stumbling, over the rough field. Will had a bad feeling, a sick presentiment that grew as he neared.

One of the Missouri troopers had torn open Steve Staszewsky's shirt and was administering CPR. He paused, pressed his ear to the bare chest. In complete bewilderment, he said, ''Nothing. Absolutely nothing.''

''Don't stop!''

''We won't. We won't stop. But the guy's dead.''

''He can't be dead! No one was near him; no one laid a glove on him!''

Sweat was running down the trooper's face. He motioned to his partner, and they switched without breaking rhythm. He sat back on his heels, gasped to Will, "It's crazy! There's not a mark!"

The driver of the second Jeep was being sick in the bushes. He came back, wiping his mouth, and said, "He can't be dead! My God, he was just walking over to me, bitching about dirtying his suit. Then he—he sort of—gurgled and grabbed his chest. And there he was. On the ground! I don't believe it! D'you suppose it was his heart?"

Steve Staszewsky lay looking up at them, an expression of faint surprise in his open eyes. Linda made a small noise and turned away. Will patted her shoulder, but it was automatic. His mind was elsewhere.

The sheriff was on the radio, calling for an ambulance to meet them at the foot of the bluff. One of the deputies had hauled a blanket out of somewhere; he brought it over and put it down. Will was torn between staying out of the affair and a compulsion to know. The compulsion was stronger.

He shoved his Massey-Ferguson cap to the back of his head and knelt beside the laboring policeman. Not interrupting the rhythm, he pushed his hand under Staszewsky's back.

Steve's suitcoat was cashmere, soft and silky.

That was all he felt.

He withdrew the hand, tugged out a swatch of shirttail and pushed again. Steve's back was hard and still warm.

But this time there was something else.

The trooper was saying irritably, "What the hell do you think you're doing? Get out of the way!"

Then he saw Will's red hand.

He stopped. He said, "Oh, God."

They rolled Steve over on his stomach, his arms flopping like a doll's, and tore up his suit coat.

The raw silk lining was wet. The shirt was very wet. The fit, tanned back was smeared with blood.

The Jeep driver made for the bushes again. The trooper was bewildered, "But there was nothing there—nothing!"

There was no pleasure for Will in being right—not in this sort of thing, not anymore. "There wouldn't be any blood. Not at first."

The sheriff had returned and was kneeling with them around the body. "What the hell?"

"I'm not sure." But that was a lie. Will was sure, he was just being tactful again. Better let someone else be sure too. "Feel between his shoulder blades. Easy. Don't hurry. It'll be small."

Will was conscious of the circle of faces around him and very little breathing. A sort of catch in time. The sheriff's fingers moved, getting bloody, up and down. Then he froze.

"You're right. A piece of metal. Like the head of a finishing nail."

Will nodded. "Yeah." His haunches ached. He rose to his feet and looked through the bewildered knot of men to Slit, who was sitting quietly in the Jeep, flanked by deputies.

Slit returned his stare. There was no animosity in his iron face. "You're still damned smart, Westerson. How come you quit?"

Because I'd had enough of cockroaches like you.

But Will didn't say it. He just turned back to the sheriff, who was pulling Steve's shirt and coat back down, getting to his own feet. He looked stunned. Nodding to his men to use the blanket as a stretcher, he said grimly to Will, "He did it?"

"He did it."

"Where the hell did he have it hidden? We were so sure he was clean!"

Will shrugged. "Somewhere he could reach in a hurry. It wouldn't take up much more room than a long, skinny push-pin. Staszewsky probably never really knew when it hit him." He added with a sort of painful reluctance, "The guy is very good at what he does."

The sheriff was going on as though he hadn't even been listening, "Staszewsky wasn't on the level. Elman said he wasn't on the level; he warned me he might show up. I wouldn't let him get close to the prisoner. I thought I was watching him . . . '' He stopped, cursed harshly, and smacked the side of the Jeep with an impotent fist, calling Slit every vile name he could think of. He knew quite a few.

Slit sat impervious in the Jeep, staring straight ahead, saying nothing.

He said nothing all the way back to town. When they were through with him for a while, when they opened a cell and thrust him in it, he tested the mattress on the cot, lay down gently because of his bandaged ribs, and shut his eyes. He had to think.

If there was a way to survive, he'd find it.

If there was a way . . .

Chapter Nineteen

AT THE BOTTOM of the bluff, the sheriff took pity on the forlorn young woman in the torn sweatshirt, found Will a car, and told him to take her home. She could, the sheriff said, come down and make her statement when she wasn't opening up all their sinuses.

His attempt at humor was rewarded by a watery smile. Will shepherded her into the spare Oldsmobile, slid under the wheel, and headed across the valley to the river.

She was twisting dirty fingers together in her lap. He laid his on hers briefly. "Buck up. The world hasn't ended. In fact, I feel a hundred per cent better than I did two hours ago."

She looked at her watch, then back at him. Blankly. In disbelief. She said in a husky voice, "Two hours! It's only eight-thirty. It seems like a lifetime. I still can't—can't grasp it all. I can't believe it happened to me. To me! Other people—but not me."

"It did. It did happen. It was sheer chance, but it happened, Linda. He is a pretty simple guy in many ways."

"Simple!" It burst from her. "He's crazy! He tried to kill me. He did kill that other man!"

"For one simple reason. Survival. He thought you could blow his cover. A cover he had jealously protected for years. His primary value was going down the tube."

"But I couldn't!"

"He didn't know that. And the fact that it was all a wasted effort must have had a particular sting." He stopped at the intersection, then followed a truckload of apples onto the bridge.

"He was trying to protect his professional credibility. All you had to do was stay alive."

She wasn't smiling. "And the poor man he did kill?"

Now he wasn't smiling, either. "With him, it was different. With Steve Staszewsky, Slit was trying to stay alive." He glanced at her, and his eyes were sober. "Ten to one, in Steve's custody Slit wouldn't have made it back to St. Louis."

"You can't mean that!"

"I can mean it. I just can't prove it. Thank God, I don't have to, either. Someone else will, though."

He got a chance to whip around the apple truck. The two kids dangling their legs on top waved and hooted derisively. Not even wanting to talk about Steve Staszewsky, he went on, "And you, lady, you must have had some efficient angel on your shoulder! Because I know Slit was at the airport yesterday morning when you landed without your glasses. I saw him, and I'll bet you weren't far out of his sight from then on."

She shuddered. "I never saw *him*!"

"*You* weren't looking for him. But I also know he followed you to Bellam's, because I saw him again at the yard sale—yet, like an idiot, I still couldn't put enough facts together to know why he was there. All of which reminds me—my dummy act cost me seven bucks. I hope you like Depression glass."

Her eyes were on the broad, shining river—eyes that turned the chopping waves to pewter satin. And she wasn't listening. She was thinking, instead, *He must have been close, so close. In the closet he could have reached out and touched me. He did almost grab me last night in the lane. And how many other times when I didn't even know . . .*

She started to shake. And she couldn't stop. She put her dirty hands to her face and said through chattering teeth, "Oh, I'm sorry—I'm sorry—"

"Oh, hush!" He put out his big arm, gathering her close in a huddle against his warm side. "It's over. You're all right. That's the thing to remember. The Number One thing. And right here, by the way, is where we all pulled over and watched you do your air show.''

She raised her head, startled, to meet his eyes.

''You're good,'' he said soberly. ''Damned good. I mean it, Linda. I'd like to watch you sometime when you aren't just trying to stay alive.''

Suddenly ridiculously happy, ''Oh, Will, next week at my dad's—'' Then she remembered the tattered Cub. Her lip quivered, and tears began to flow again.

''Now stop that!'' He sounded exasperated. ''The Cub will be fine! I told you! Good grief, woman, I took a landing light in her belly once and flew two hundred miles more after patching the rip with duct tape!''

They were rounding the bend in the highway by the motel. The sun was shining brightly, his arm was warm and tight, and he'd just said he liked her flying. She was starting to sit up and feel better.

Then it was over.

''Doris!'' Will abruptly pulled the car over to the side of the road. It took a moment for Linda to connect the name with the tall, jeans-clad woman they'd just passed, but when it did, she stiffened. Will leaned over her and threw open the door on her side of the car.

''Doris! What are you doing out here?''

''Walking!'' The word came out in an explosion and was followed by a stream of invective that had to do with Tony's origins and the fact that he'd taken her car. When she reached them, her eyes were blue-black with anger. They widened and she stopped in her tracks when she caught sight of Linda.

''Get in.'' Will ordered tersely. When Doris didn't move, Will shouted this time, ''Get in!''

Doris looked at Linda. Linda gave a small, frozen shrug. Doris threw her small bag in the back and joined them on the front seat. Will concentrated on his driving and the two women eyed each other warily. Finally, Doris broke the uncomfortable silence, ''I tried to find you last night. After Will threw me out . . . '' she shot him a quick glance, hoping he appreciated the small fib, ''Well, I did find your apartment.''

''Oh,'' said Linda. It was the best she could do.

''Oh?'' echoed Will, but his was a question. ''And?'' he added. Linda's apartment was on the east side of town and they'd just found Doris on the west side.

''And I found Tony there, making himself comfortable. He gave me some song and dance . . . '' She took a deep breath. This was no fun. ''Anyway, to make a long story short, we ended up going to a motel, and in the middle of the night, he took my car and blew. So there you have it, the whole glorious story. I was walking to get his car.''

''I'll take you,'' said Will magnanimously. ''You know how accommodating I am.''

He could feel Linda against his arm, very stiff and very still. Okay. She had about four blocks in which to think about it. Tony, huh?

Doris, having stopped her tirade, was sniffing the air. ''Where have you been driving this thing? Through a sewer? Something smells!''

''Yes. Doesn't it?'' Will answered dryly. ''Linda got thrown up on this morning. I was taking her home to get cleaned up. Oh, I believe you ladies have met.''

Neither of them dignified that with an answer. He smiled, albeit a little grimly, and wheeled into the parking area of Linda's apartment. ''Which car?''

''The Datsun,'' said Doris.

''He has good taste,'' said Will, and pulled alongside. ''But, I knew that. Didn't I?''

Doris rather crisply told him to put that remark in a place normally unavailable to sunshine and climbed out. ''Thanks for the ride,'' she said. ''I guess. I have a date in St. Louis. To cook spaghetti for a guy I know. You two sort it out between yourselves.''

She got into the Datsun, started it with a burst of noise that made Will flinch, then drove out of the lot and out of sight.

Then it was quiet again. Very. Linda was suffering. Will knew it. He was rather pleased about it. It was her turn.

But when she swallowed, started to say in a shaky voice, "Will, Tony—just—turned up—I didn't know—"

He looked at her squarely. Then, his voice over hers, he said in a gentle tone, "It would seem we have had this conversation before. In reverse."

Miserably she whispered, "I know. I know that. But I just want you to understand—"

Then he stopped her in a different way. He leaned over, took her dirty face in both hands and put his mouth on hers. He felt her lips flutter against his, stop, and go soft and sweet, like warm silk. Her arms went around him, and they were loving arms, pulling them together.

It was quite obvious that words were not necessary, but he wanted to say them anyway. He slid his mouth to her warm throat, kissed it, said against the side of her head, "Listen good. Outside this car is a beautiful, new day. A new day. You hear me? And I think I love you. Can we go from here—from this point? Can we, Linda?"

That was no problem. The first of those came a few moments later when he said shakily, "Hey, babe—whoa—we'd better ease off. The first time I make love to you it's going to be long and lovely and unhurried and very private. Not in full view of your neighbors."

She smiled. "What do you think's been going on for ten minutes?"

Loftily he answered, "We've not been making love. We've been necking. There's a difference. If you don't know what it is, make an appointment and I'll demonstrate."

He was right, of course, but she couldn't afford to let him get away with such a smart-aleck remark. "I hope you understand that I'm going along with this just to have a place to ribstitch repairs on the Cub. It's a little hard to get an airplane into an apartment."

He snorted. "For all you know, I'm just going along with this to get my airplane back!"

Zingo. The Big Problem.

Startled, they eyed each other warily.

Yet, it would be a problem only if they allowed it to be.

With two very stubborn people, not allowing it to be would take a little doing. More than a little. A lot.

Will whistled. "Hey, Babe," he said, "we're in for some really good times, you know."

"Well, then—let's get started."

If you have enjoyed this book and would like to receive details of other Walker publications, please write to:

Judy Sullivan Books
Walker and Company
720 Fifth Avenue
New York, NY 10019